D1582670

This bc

ABSOLUTE ELIZABETH
Book Two of the 'Elizabeth I' trilogy

Released from a life spent in constant terror of death from her enemies, the young Queen Elizabeth mounts the throne of England. She reveals an inborn instinct for government, a natural flair for politics and an unerring judge of character. She is truly herself for the first time. Her headstrong behaviour with handsome Lord Robert Dudley causes scandal; she allows her temper full sway. The suspicion of murder brushes her, but her many suitors are undeterred. Cool and cunning, Elizabeth brings England prosperity and makes herself viewed with caution all over Europe.

Books by Joanna Dessau
Published by The House of Ulverscroft:

THE GREY GOOSE
THE BLACKSMITH'S DAUGHTER
CROWN OF SORROWS
NO WAY OUT
THE CONSTANT LOVER
TAKE NOW, PAY LATER
ALL OR NOTHING

ELIZABETH I TRILOGY
THE RED-HAIRED BRAT
(Book One)

JOANNA DESSAU

ABSOLUTE ELIZABETH

Complete and Unabridged

ULVERSCROFT
Leicester

First published in Great Britain in 1978

First Large Print Edition
published 2000

British Library CIP Data

Dessau, Joanna
    Absolute Elizabeth.—Large print ed.—
    Ulverscroft large print series: general fiction
    1. Large type books
    I. Title
    823.9'14 [F]

    ISBN 0–7089–4166–4

Published by
F. A. Thorpe (Publishing) Ltd.
Anstey, Leicestershire
Set by Words & Graphics Ltd.
Anstey, Leicestershire
Printed and bound in Great Britain by
T. J. International Ltd., Padstow, Cornwall

This book is printed on acid-free paper

To my loved and lovely son
NICK SALOMAN

Prologue

21st January 1603

Here at Richmond am I at last. Jesus, but my rheum grows none the better! I sniff and sneeze, cough and spit with it like any old goody, Queen Elizabeth of England though I be. I vow my nose is raw with rubbing. I lie upon my daybed, almost atop the fire, and still my old bones shiver. Ach, I hate old age and ugliness, helplessness and illness, and I suffer from all four, poor old beldame that I am. Nigh on seventy years is a great age, for few folk live past their fifties, falling victim to plagues, poxes and sweats, so harried are we poor mortals. I have been luckier, having reigned in good fortune for well-nigh a lifetime, my rule extending over more than forty-four years. Why, those who were but new-born when I came to the Throne are grandparents now and I a withered ancient whose time runs out apace. I fear God will not grant me much longer upon His sweet earth, my England to succour. I may never

1

see another summer.

Outside it is grey and wild, with rain in the wind, cold and gloomy like the heart in my bosom. Hey, such a fuss did I cause by my decision to move hither at this time of the year! So many arguments and protestations put forward to dissuade me! The roads would be impassable for mud, the careware carts would stick up to the axles, how would the gear be got to Richmond, and so on and so on. Poor souls, my courtiers and ladies wished to stay snug at White Hall until the spring. But to move I was determined, for Dr. John Dee, who has never advised me ill, had urged me to go, saying: 'Beware of White Hall, for 'tis parlous cold and chill for you, my Queen. You must take care lest your rheum grow worse. Go to Richmond,' said he, ' 'tis a warm winter box to shelter you in your old age.' Old age, forsooth, the saucy wight, and he older than I by six years!

Still, we came here easily enough by water, although it was cold, with an icy wind whipping off the water, seeking a way through my furs. I broke the journey at Putney to call upon old John Lacy, the cloth merchant, my good friend these many years. He was greatly pleased to see me and offered me hot spiced wine which I enjoyed, needing the warmth thereof in my body.

'Be sure to keep you warm at Richmond, dearest Majesty,' he advised me. ' 'Tis desperate cold and treacherous weather. I like not to think of you a-travelling. You must get there before dark, and not waste your time chattering to me.'

'Time, is it John? I have not much left to waste, methinks. But you are right, I must get on my way. Come, my lords and ladies, to the boats, for I must be off!' I gave John my hand and he knelt to kiss it. 'Farewell, old friend. If God wills, I will call upon you later in the year.'

So we took up our journey again and I was glad enough to descry the towers of rosy Richmond appearing round the bend of the Thames. Gladder still as we slid past the tall gatehouse straddling the tow-path and tied up at the steps. But we had made good speed and most of the furnishings had been brought by water also, so quick comfort for us all was assured.

Ay, it is warmer here indeed. Mayhap the place is well sheltered or catches more sun. Mayhap 'tis better built than my other palaces. For sure, White Hall, though handsome, is a draughty hole, no matter what I do to rectify it. It has wondrous large fireplaces, but the heat goes straight up the chimneys like a lost soul in search of salvation from Heaven. Here at Richmond, one reaps the full benefit from a fire. It must be in the chimneys that the secret lies. I will look into the matter of the stacks of White Hall upon my return there. It is work long overdue.

My grandfather Henry VII was fond of Richmond, though it was called Sheen when he came to it. To show his liking for the palace, he had it rebuilt after it was ruined by a great fire when my own father was but seven years old. My grandsire renamed it Richmond after his Earldom of Richmond in Yorkshire and so it has been called ever after. Moreover, I have a system of piped water here, also the excellent new-fangled jakes constructed by Boy Jack Harington, my godson. This is a marvellous machine with a shaped wooden seat and water that flushes all muck down, clean and odourless, so that I may void myself in comfort, without recourse to a stinking close-stool, nor need I struggle up a winding stair to a smelly garderobe, which is discomfortable to a poor old woman with a rheum.

Also, there is an especial appeal about Richmond on a windy day, for atop the many towers and turrets are a myriad weather-vanes. The gusts blow through these and tinkle a thousand aery harmonies like none

4

heard elsewhere. 'Tis lovely and strange, like music from another world. Ay, Richmond has much to recommend it. I will stay here until I move to Nonsuch in the spring. It will suit me well, and I can rest in comfort, turning my mind to memories of myself as a new-made Queen when I and my world were young.

1

UNDOUBTED QUEEN

17th November 1558 to 15th January 1559

It was daybreak on the 17th of November 1558, and I was twenty-five years old, two months and ten days. I had arisen betimes and taken a manchet of white bread and a mug of ale to break my fast.

' 'Tis a pleasant day in the sunshine, Kat,' I said to my one-time governess and now beloved friend. 'Give me my hat and a cloak and I will walk outdoors awhile.'

My tall, slight figure wrapped in a fur-lined rose-coloured velvet cloak, my red hair bundled carelessly under my pink, broad-leaved garden hat, I went outside into the chill air. I wandered about, scarce knowing what I did, for I knew in my heart that my sister Queen Mary was no more. I felt my life opening out before me like the dawn as I stood beneath a great oak, its few remaining leaves shrivelled now and autumn-brown; its branches dark against the clear sky. As I stood, I saw the Lords of the

Council, cloaked and urgent, hurrying across the dew-wet grass to kneel before me.

'Majesty,' they said. 'The Queen is dead. Long live the Queen.' As they knelt, so did I also. The reason of my birth was upon me and I bowed before the only One now higher than myself.

'*A domine factum, est et mirabilis in oculis nostris!*' said I. 'This is the work of the Lord, and it is marvellous in our eyes.'

I was Queen. Queen Elizabeth of England by the will of mine own dear English people who wanted me and no other. For this had I been born, rendered homeless, endured terror, loneliness and hardships. The stone that the builders had rejected had become the headstone of the corner, and England should feel the support, love and concern of a Queen who was that headstone.

I arose from my knees and those solemn men did too. We gazed at one another, panting slightly as if we had just recovered from a hard race. So we had then, and what a race! We had passed the pikes and come out safe on the other side. There was the oak tree, its branches reaching out over my head, there was the fretful November sky. The grass lay green beneath my feet, the little breeze blew chill about me, the old red brick of Hatfield Palace rose beyond the

8

gardens to my left; all was exactly as it had been but a few moments before. Yet we all knew that nothing would ever be the same again. I lifted my chin, feeling my body relax as I smiled round at them staring so earnestly at me. Then William Cecil silently handed me my sister Queen Mary's black and gold betrothal ring. I took it in my palm, closing my fingers tightly about it. Here is all the proof I need, I thought. This means that Mary has gone from the world we all know so well; this little ring tells me that I am Queen more powerfully than any words or proclamation can do. Raising my eyes to the spaces above, I breathed a silent prayer for her soul. Silent stood those grave-faced men awaiting my pleasure.

'Come, sirs,' I said quietly, giving Cecil my hand upon his arm, 'let us go in. There is much to do.'

The rest of that day of my accession passed as a confused mass of images upon my brain. I mind the thrilling tension, the ceaseless babble of voices punctuated by excited bursts of laughter within the palace, the bells ringing and jangling day-long without; the hurry-scurry to and fro of servants, messengers, ladies and gentlemen, Councillors, of lap-dogs under feet, wine spilled in the rushes as someone's arm was jogged in the constant movement. I remained fairly calm, for I felt curiously apart from my surroundings, almost on another plane, outside myself, translated. And still the bells pealed out their joyful tidings, not only through that wondrous Thursday, but through most of the night as well.

They still ring for me upon the 17th November and have done since that day, every year of my reign. Will I hear them next November? Ah, that is a question none can answer, save only God, and He remains silent upon such matters. But I have had more than one warning, the latest and worst being the removal of the most precious jewel I possess. I mean my Coronation Ring, the ring that wedded me to England. It had grown so tight upon my old finger, and caused me so much pain thereby, that I had to submit to its being sawn off. I tell you, 'twas like losing a limb or the finger itself. My heart bleeds yet from the wound and will go on bleeding from the severed bond 'twixt me and my England. The loss of my ring brings great melancholy upon my spirit and an ugly foreboding that my future is short. Well, Death will have to fight for me, for I shall be no easy conquest, not I.

So I lie, warm upon my day-bed by the fire in the winter parlour at Richmond, cushions at my back, my body covered with a fur quilt, dreaming my dreams and thinking my thoughts this bleak January evening. My ladies sit in a group round a brazier at the far end of the chamber. I can hear their voices chatting quietly, for they wish not to disturb me. Little do they know that in my mind's eye I see the figure of a young woman, scarce more than a girl, flung face down across a bed in a dark chamber, weeping sad and woeful, for her dead sister, also a Queen. Yea, I wept sore for Mary. She had given me my greatest wish and died in so doing, she was my sister — how could I not weep? But my tears had to be for the hours of night, for my people would rather see me radiant and smiling, a picture of all they wished in a Sovereign, and 'fore God, there was a mort of things to do before ever I reached London.

During these days all was bustle and running back and forth, and I in the midst giving my orders as if I had ruled all my life. Indeed, I held my first Council meeting in the Great Hall of Hatfield Palace, but three days after my accession, and greatly did I enjoy the exercise.

William Cecil, he who had been at my side, in spirit, during my brother's reign and my sister's, now was with me in the flesh, all subterfuge cast happily aside. I made him my Chief Secretary of State to take pains for me and my realm.

'See now, Mr. Secretary,' I said, my voice ringing easily through the crowded hall, 'I know you to be both faithful and incorruptible. I know you will advise me despite any wishes I may have privately, and I tell you now before all, that if you shall know anything necessary to be declared to me of secrecy, you shall show it to myself only and assure yourself that I shall keep taciturnity thereunto.'

It was a promise and I kept it always.

Cecil was about thirty-eight at this time. Slight, thin and pale in body, he was a giant in mind and ability. Like me, he had come into his own. My fond name for him was 'Spirit', and rightly so, for 'twas his own that had saved me from almost certain death on more than one occasion when mine enemies had closed about me.

I made Kat Ashley First Lady of the Bedchamber, and who better than she, my more-than-mother? She had been with me since I was but four years old, first as a Lady Governess, now as beloved friend. Well-born she was, being a Champernowne of Tywardreath in Cornwall and sister-in-law to Sir Anthony Denny, one-time Privy

Councillor to my father. I loved her dearer than any I knew. Her husband John I made Keeper of the Queen's Jewels; Tom Parry, my faithful cofferer, I knighted and made Treasurer of the Household. In that office, his troublesome accounts, which never would tally, could be done by underlings. And dear Blanche Parry, so full of years and wisdom, who had loved me since I was a babe, I made Keeper of the Royal Books at Windsor. My good, brave uncle, Lord William Howard, I created a Privy Councillor and to the Earl of Arundel I gave the same appointment also.

It was wondrous, it was heady, but my mind remained as clear as crystal. I felt no strangeness nor indecision in the making of these appointments; after all, I had had time enough to decide as to their suitability, and time showed the rightness of my choice. And what of he who had arrived at Hatfield even before this first Council meeting? What of Robert Dudley, friend of my childhood and would-be lover? I had not set eyes upon him since my imprisonment in the Tower, four years agone, when we were both captives and I in danger of sneaking death. Wed though he was, he had told me of the love he bore for me, then, and I had confessed mine for him, retaining my maidenhead more by luck than design. He burst upon me at Hatfield on the very heels of the Lords who brought the news of my sister's death. Riding a white charger he came, all afire, prating of Fate and Destiny, to throw himself at my feet. Right brave and bonny he looked too, his bright black eyes fixed upon mine as he knelt before me.

'My Liege!' he cried. 'My beautiful Queen, Sovereign of this land and my heart!' He laid his long, brown hand upon the breast of his tawney velvet doublet whilst holding mine in the other. I heard the scandalised breaths drawn all around me at this bold and extravagant behaviour, and, looking under my lashes, caught the shocked glances flicked from one Councillor to another. Inwardly did I laugh most uproariously, but outwardly, although my eyes danced, I permitted but a small smile to escape me.

'Dearest Rob,' I said clearly, 'well pleased am I to see you and hear your welcome words. I am told that you outdistanced all upon the road by your horsemanship.'

'Fast and furious! My heart would not let me wait.'

'Skilful riding too,' I answered. 'Ever had you a knack with animals, did you not, Rob?'

'Ay indeed, sweet Majesty, and right glad am I to put it to your service.'

14

'You shall be rewarded,' said I, smiling upon him, 'my Master of the Horse!'

He sprang to his feet, aflame with pride and delight, his arms flung wide as if he would embrace me, but I shook my head very slightly to warn him off, for already I could hear faint, but outraged cluckings, and whilst I cared not a rap for that, the dignity of my Queenship was strong upon me. 'Twould have looked most unseemly for the Sovereign of England to be swept unresisting into the arms of a subject, and he a married man. But oh, it warmed my heart! Some said it was mere vulgar place-seeking and only to be expected of a Dudley upstart, but I knew better. I knew him as if he had been mine own self. We had what is called Synastria, or star-sympathy, being star-twins as we were. Why, when I was so sore in debt, shut away at Woodstock, Rob sold some of his lands secretly and gave the receipts to me to help me in my difficulties. I had not asked him to do so, 'twould have brought him no preferment to do so, for I was out of favour and regarded with suspicion and distrust by my sister Queen Mary. Nay, 'twas from his own kind heart and touched mine own deeply. We had a kinship between us that naught but death of the body could sever, and not even then, for he is in his grave now and I miss him and yearn for him still.

Upon the 23rd of November we took horse for London, to Lord North's house in the Barbican hard by the Charter-house. Upwards of a thousand ladies and gentlemen accompanied me thither and I rode at the head of this great procession, the sound of the horses' hooves being audible miles away. At times I felt as if I must be asleep and dreaming, yet I was never more awake in my life. All along the way there was wild pealing of bells, shouts and uproar. The country folk ran after my horse, some tried to catch the bridle, and I would suffer none to stay them. My people. They were mine and I was theirs and all would be accord between us. I could have embraced and kissed each one, so did the love flow out from me towards them. They knew it, ay, and they shouted theirs for me. 'Elizabeth for ever! Our Elizabeth for ever! At last, at last, most dear Lady!' all the way to London. It was more than I had ever known, in spite of my certainty that I was much loved and had it shown me by my countrymen over and over again, all through my life.

'Christ!' gasped Kat Ashley as we dismounted in the courtyard of my Lord North's house. 'The whole country is running mad.

Did you ever hear such crazy uproar? Do they mean to ring bells and yell for ever? And we are not yet truly within the City! I cannot imagine what it will be like when your Grace rides to the Tower.'

'I can!' I cried, all afire with laughter and excitement. 'It will be like Heaven, Kat — my Heaven here on earth! But hush now, here comes Lord North to welcome us and I must behave Queenly.'

We stayed at Lord North's for some several days and I held assemblies there to meet those who would meet me. Hey, but candles blazed, torches flared and people laughed and chattered far into the night, with music, dancing and merriment.

Kat was much put about at the plainness of my wardrobe, but what mattered it, said I, all a-laughing. I was the highest in the land and could set fashions as I wished, go barefoot as I wanted, appear in rags as I list, and all would admire and follow me. There would be time enough, I said, for rich dresses and glitter.

'Time enough!' I cried, arms flung wide. 'A life-time, Kat! See, I have Lord North's best chamber, his house is mine for as long as I wish, his servants, his duty, his loyalty, Kat! All, all is mine. England is mine.'

Suddenly, my laughter quieted and I sank

on to the great oaken bed with its purple silk coverlet broidered in gold and bordered with fur. I stared up at the tester hung with tapestries, my glance wandering up to the carven plaster ceiling, flickering pink and shadowed in the firelight from the wide hearth with his Lordship's arms wrought above. Nay, thought I, this is more than mere possession. It is a sacred trust.

'England is mine,' I breathed. 'God send me grace to rule and preserve her to the end of my days, even as He has seen fit to raise me to this high place.'

'Amen to that,' responded Kat devoutly, falling to her knees. And so we prayed a space, after which I rose and went down to the throng awaiting me. And still the bells rang and the people sang and shouted, day after day.

Here, to Lord North's house, came Count De Feria to present his credentials to me as Queen. As soon as I saw him struggling through the press of people, dressed in his black velvet with the Spanish Order of the Golden Fleece sparkling with diamonds around his neck and on his breast, I waved to him to come forward, smiling and stripping off my glove as I did so, that he might kiss my hand. At once the crowd parted to make way for him to come to me. Bowing with many a flourish, he was the model of a correct and formal Ambassador.

'My good Count De Feria,' I said pleasantly, 'I am delighted to receive the Ambassador of my cherished brother of Spain.'

Once more he bowed, this time in acknowledgement. 'And I, dearest Majesty, am here only to discover how your kingly brother may serve you.'

Very different, thought I, from your pompous patronising, earlier, at Hatfield. Now all oil and butter, by my faith, and where is the sting in the tail of the message? I was soon to find out, for, looking me straight in the eye, De Feria said: 'Sovereign Lady, my royal master desires you to use great care in religious matters. These are his chiefest concern and he would know your mind upon the subject. Have you aught to say of it?'

A fine time to ask that, at one of my first public assemblies, with every eye upon me and every ear a-cock for me to declare for Catholics or Protestants and so label myself for ever as upon one side or the other! I had spent most of my life, hereunto, doing the exact opposite and was not to be drawn now. Oh no indeed, Master De Feria, I am not the little, weak woman you imagine, thought I, as you will swiftly discover. Two can play at that game, my dear man, flash your black eyes never so fierily! So I kept my face calm and innocent and answered with maidenly gravity.

'My mind is that it would indeed be bad of me to forget God who has been so good to me.'

Oho, I saw his mouth tighten and the spark flame in his dark eyes. I widened my own very slightly as I gave him back stare for stare. A breath of relief and approbation fluttered from appreciative lips in the throng. I had sidestepped that impasse very neatly. 'Twas but the first engagement; our foils were buttoned and none yet knew my true mettle. De Feria, looking furious, bowed again, but he could do no more than look, for he was forced to keep upon good terms with me, the reason being that his little Spanish master wished him to sue, as his proxy, for my hand in marriage. It would never do to quarrel so early in the game, he knew, and perhaps lose the rich prize of England for Spain.

'Mayhap it would be possible to speak with your Grace upon this matter at another time,' he said at last, in a grating voice.

'Most assuredly, my dear Count,' I answered affably. 'I will send two of my Council to summon you to my presence when 'tis convenient.' That should settle him, I reflected. But he tried again.

'May I ask which two, Majesty?' He was hoping for sympathisers, of course. Well, I would scotch that.

'Indeed you may,' I trilled. 'I will send Sir William Cecil and Sir Thomas Parry, two of my trustiest advisers.'

I near laughed at his imperfectly concealed glare of exasperation as, with compressed lips, he fought to subdue his natural feelings and behave correctly as a Spanish grandee should when upon international business with a female of whom, although a Queen, he strongly disapproved. I knew his opinion of Cecil and Parry. He regarded both as naught but a pair of rascally thatchgallows and realised that he would get nowhere with either. I knew, too, what he thought of me. To him, I was a heretic bastard of an upstart, usurping house, with no notion of the niceties of diplomatic behaviour and deplorably lacking in even the vestiges of good breeding; a tricky, dissimulating, obviously unmanageable woman. He was soon to realise that he would get nowhere with me, neither.

I held daily meetings while I stayed with my kind host, the first of many hosts to entertain me in this way. There was a deputation of judges come there, as I recall, and to these I spoke myself. Cecil had apprised me of the sad state into which the courts of the land had fallen. He, being a lawyer himself, was able to put the case clearly to me, saying that the standard of the courts could only be raised if the judges were paid more money to elevate their status. This would attract more honourable and high-thinking men, he said, and do away with the abuses that were rife.

'Sir William Cecil has told me of your case,' I said, addressing them from the dais upon which I sat. 'I will see to it at once that your monies are increased. And for this service that I do you, so you must do one for me. I hear that there are evil-doers in your profession that care not for honour and justice. These must be rooted out. I charge all of you who sit here as ambassadors of justice in my name, to have a care over my people. They are *my* people. Every man oppresseth them and spoileth them without mercy. See unto them, see unto them, for they are my charge!'

My voice rang through the hall and my heart must have been in the sound of it, for some of them actually wept while others fell on their knees. When they had bowed themselves out, I turned to Cecil. 'Expedite it, my dear man,' I said. 'I would not have them think I am say all and do naught.'

He smiled at me fondly, proudly. 'You will be the greatest monarch we have ever known, sweet Madam, for you are above all, yet above nothing.'

'Nay, you forget my father. I could not be greater than he, William! He was a very god on earth, a prince of power and plenty. I could not be greater than he.'

'Oh, already most incomparably so, dearest Lady. Infinitely so. You have so subtle a magic that you cast a spell in your very shadow. Oh yes indeed,' as I shook my head in disbelief. 'We have all felt it. Even Ambassador Simon Renard said that you had a 'spirit full of incantation,' and he was one of your greatest foes during your sister's reign.'

'Said he that?' I cried. 'Why, in those days I was sick and pale, harried from place to place like a stray dog! Renard wished me dead so that I could never become Queen and thus an enemy of Spain. He almost persuaded my sister to kill me and lucky was I that she could not bring herself to do it. Even then you did your best for me, did you not? Even before that, when my brother was alive, you saved me from Black John of

Northumberland, dost recall?'

He nodded, remembering well those dark and dangerous days when he had stood my friend, in secret, and kept me from so much harm from my Rob's own father, the wily and menacing Duke of Northumberland, who had sought to put Mary and me out of the way so that he could rule my brother and England. He was gone to his account now, for my sister Mary had seen to that and sent him to the block when she had become Queen. She could do no less with such a formidable adversary.

'That is all behind us now,' said Cecil. 'We are in the full light of noonday and you are the sun in our heaven.'

Oh, my father! I thought. Feared, beloved being, you who had scant time for any save your adored little son, would you not now be proud of your younger daughter, your red-haired brat, your rejected, neglected Bess? Would you not now smile upon her, praise her, and love her for evermore? Would you not now — at last? Shrugging my shoulders, I sighed. Well-a-day, regrets were useless, their time was past; the present and the future were mine and I must look to those.

★ ★ ★

24

I had a purple velvet riding habit when I rode to the Tower to take up my official residence there. Kat and my ladies wrought it up from one that was given me as a gift by one of the notables at the assemblies. I was right pleased to have it, for my gowns were dead plain, me having had to act the meek mouse with a mind above such fripperies as pretty robes while my sister had been alive. All I possessed were well-worn, and none was fit for such an occasion, so the purple velvet was more than welcome. With the bodice taken in and the skirt lengthened it looked very well when I tried it on.

'A truly regal colour,' said my cousin Katey Knollys, with much satisfaction. 'It sets off your pearly paleness excellent well, dear Madam.'

I was glad to have my cousin Katey with me. She was daughter to my mother's sister, Mary Boleyn, and may have been my half-sister too, for all I know. She was but a few years older than I, gentle, sweet-faced and merry, wed to a gent called Francis Knollys over whom I had some reservations in the matter of his religious feelings. He was a red-hot Protestant, most militant, being one of those who expected me to take up the cause of religious reformation and wave it as a banner. This I had no intention of doing, as he would discover. We had suffered too much o' religion in the past many years and sore trouble it had caused. However, I gave Sir Francis a place on the Privy Council, for he was a trustworthy fellow and loyal. My cousin Katey I made a gentlewoman of the Privy Chamber in order to have her near me. I enjoyed her company and that of her older brother, Henry Carey, whom I judged as a very clever and far-seeing man who would do well. He was remarkably like me in feature and I was almost certain that he was my half-brother, for his mother and my father had been lovers at the time of his birth. Half-blood or no, he and Katey were my full cousins and I liked to have them both about me. It gave me a feeling of great comfort to find these close relatives after my lonely childhood, relatives who shared a likeness of feature and temperament with me. So ran my thoughts as I smoothed the skirts of my purple gown, smiling absently the while.

'Heavens, but it will be cold!' cried Kat, recalling me to everyday affairs. 'The 28th of November is near unto full winter, thou knowest. You should wear a hat, my darling, indeed you should.'

'Oh ay, there is a hat with the gown. I had forgot,' I said. ' 'Tis broad-leaved, with an elegant white feather. Here, bring it for me to try.' I set it upon my head, and in truth, I made a brave show. Kat and Katey clapped their hands in admiration.

'But you should have a scarf, or some such, about your neck against the wind,' fussed Kat. 'We cannot have you catching a rheum and losing your voice.'

'Well, then, find me one and I will wear it,' I said amiably, 'for I think that, above all things, a rheum is the most unattractive for anyone to have about them. I would wish to look the best I can, so that the people will see me happy and healthy and be proud that I am their Queen.'

'God send us fair weather then. Come, my love, you should be abed against the excitements of the morrow. Shall I call your women now?' Kat was pulling curtains and shaking pillows.

'Ay, do that,' I answered lazily, smiling at her. 'Kat, I think I may rule England, but you still seek to rule me, do you not?'

'And ever shall while I live,' she answered briskly. 'I will return in half-an-hour with a hot posset and expect to find the Queen's Grace snug abed.'

Well, the weather was good indeed. The pale November sun shone, the air was still and not too cold, and I was up right early, at the open casement, looking across the wall of London, over the gables and gardens, to the old grey tower of St. Giles Cripplegate. There the procession was to assemble. Though early, the noise was prodigious, and when I took my place in my chariot, ready to be conveyed through the alleys to St. Giles, I was so shaken with emotion that the tears started out upon my cheeks.

In the space to the front of the church fence, the lords and ladies, and all the notables who were to take part in the procession, were already waiting, chattering excitedly, the horses stamping and tossing their heads, making the brasses jingle again. Alighting from the chariot I took horse amongst my company, and leaving the ancient church behind us, we clattered forward over the Town Ditch, through Cripplegate and into the City.

By the Cross, it was a goodly sight, with every face smiling and merry. First rode the Lord Mayor, as was his right, in his furred scarlet robes, holding my sceptre aloft in his hand. Beside him rode Garter-King-at-Arms, and behind them the Gentlemen Pensioners in red damask suits, each bearing a gilded axe; then came the heralds in their bright array, then my footmen clad in crimson and silver with the royal cypher upon their breasts. Next rode my Lord Pembroke carrying my Sword of State in a scabbard of solid gold thick with large pearls. After him trotted the serjeants-at-arms, and among them rode I in my purple velvet. Among them I was, but not crowded, and so, visible to all. Behind me came Robert all in crimson, riding a great black horse.

All so long, long ago. Forty-five years and thirty-six days, and still I see it clear as in any mirror. I hear the tin-tan of a thousand bells, the clash of arms, the roaring of many hundred throats and the booming of cannon deep in my brain. I see myself in the flower of my young womanhood, red hair falling down my back like a flame.

All along the way were bands of children singing. I drew rein and commended each one. Young schoolboys stepped forth to make welcome speeches in goodly Latin. I praised them all, for they had done their best in mine honour. At Mark Lane the sound of the Tower guns was wellnigh deafening; I never heard such shooting afore. It was continuous until I halted upon Tower Hill. Then it ceased, but still my ears rang as I looked down upon the Tower of London lying by the Thames, the home of Kings for centuries, their prison too. Once it had been mine — oh well I minded it, well indeed. My mother's also, but I would not think of that. Mayhap she watched me from Heaven and wished me well. I gazed upon the towers and turrets, the jumble of roofs, the thick curtain wall, at the mighty White Tower lifting its four pinnacles to the high, clear, pale blue sky.

'Look you,' I said, turning to Robert and pointing to the great fortress, 'some have fallen from being princes of this land to being prisoners in that place. I, myself, have risen from being a prisoner there to be a prince of this land.' And to all who could hear me, I cried: 'Let me show myself to God thankful and to men merciful!'

I was answered by a deep shout of praise and approval as I signed for the procession to go forward. On we went, my horse trotted over the drawbridge, and I was within. Not by Traitor's Gate this time, not by stealth in teeming rain, alone and in tears of misery and despair. No, by God, and never again.

At the Bell Tower I dismounted, leaving all agape and uncertain of what I would do next. I wished to re-visit my prison rooms, this time as Queen. 'Be off with you all!' I commanded. 'Dispose yourselves as you will. For me, I have a pilgrimage to make! Come, Rob, I wish you to accompany me.'

There were gasps of disapproval as I seized

30

his hand and darted within the Bell Tower, pulling him with me. We mounted the stair to my one-time prison chamber and I paced it about, gazing from each of the three windows in turn. Suddenly I span in a wild dance, singing and clapping my hands, laughing and shouting like a zany.

'Free, free, free!' I yelled. 'I am free! I can do as I like, do as I like! Hey! Hey! Hey!'

And after a moment, he joined me, twirling and stamping, mad as his Queen. He caught me about the waist, by the arms, by the hands, sometimes lifting me high in the air, sometimes turning me under his arm. 'Ho, I shall eat sweets all day!' I shrieked. 'Wear a new gown every hour, blaze with jewels, curl my hair, paint my face! Ho, ho, ho and up go we!'

'Merrily, merrily up go we!' he echoed, catching at my hair as it swung out behind me.

Sudden as I began, I stopped my dance, his arm about my waist, my hair in his hand. 'Oh Rob,' I laughed, all breathless, 'I need be meek no more — not ever! Rob, I can do exact as I like when I like, do you hear me? I may spit, I may argue, stamp, scream, swear, and there is none, not one in the whole wide world to gainsay me! And I shall do it all!'

'What, spit and swear?' he bellowed a-laughing.

'Yea, I will!' I cried.

'Stamp and scream?'

'Ay, so!' I screamed, stamping hard upon the stone floor.

'Now, by Heaven, you are a wild, wonderful witch of a woman and I love you!' he shouted. 'I love you!'

'And I love you!' I burst out.

With that, he grabbed me and kissed me like a crazy man and I kissed him, just as crazy, just as greedy. Dear God, I wanted him until my belly ached, but before he could begin to importune me I had whisked myself free and begun to run down the stairs.

'Wait, oh, wait! Bess, Bess!' he called.

'Nay, Lord Robert, remember you are married!' I cried, naughtily, over my shoulder. 'You are not for a virgin Queen.'

'My oath, but five minutes more and I would have changed all that!' He was half-angered, half-laughing.

'So I feared,' I giggled. ' 'Twould be a fine scandal to start my reign and prove all the gossips and my enemies right. So, 'tis not for us, you understand?'

He halted, his dark face ludicrous with dismay. 'What, never? Elizabeth, you cannot mean it!'

'Oh — well — leave it now, Rob. I can dally no longer. There are those who wait for me. But stay near me, my dearest. And now you must escort me to my lodgings as a well-born young gentleman should.'

'Twas intoxicating stuff, more especially to one who had never come within sniffing distance of absolute power. Now it was mine all at once. Indeed, I wonder now that I did not lose my head entirely; yet mayhap I do not really wonder, for although my nature was wild, strong and free, I never lost sight of reality, nor of my position and its responsibilities. I loved it all, the work, the worry, the devious policies I pursued, the power I wielded which grew and extended year by year, and most of all and best of all I loved my people who loved me. Oh, if I could live for ever, I would. If I could live for ever, with my faculties and energies undimmed, to keep my England safe and secure under my wing, how eagerly would I!

I know that I am the greatest ruler in the world. How could I not know it? My hand is everywhere. Yet, because I am the greatest, it follows that he who is to come after me will not be as great and will not feel for mine own as I do. It frets me sore if I let it. But I should not, for when I am gone there will be naught I can do. Leave it I must and know that I have done my best. I wedded no man, for I was already wed to England. There was a rhyme writ about it once. How did it go? *Sweet Bessie, give me thy hand* . . . was it? Ah, now I have it, one verse entire.

Here is my hand
My dear lover England.
I am thine both with mind and heart,
Forever to endure,
Thou may'st be sure,
Until death we two do part.

And that was utter truth, each same word of it. Master William Birch, who writ that piece, understood my own heart full well.

A se'ennight I stayed in the Tower, comfortable in the State Apartments which had been furbished up for me what time I lay at Lord North's house. Now I had feather beds, fur coverlets, silken pillows and rich hangings a-plenty, constant company and chatter all about me, but no time for dalliance, sweet though it might be, for many were the pressing problems that must be resolved. I wished to know them all and work their resolution myself. Daily Council meetings I held here, too. The religious question must be settled to the mutual satisfaction of both Catholics and Protestants, although to effect this would be like reaching for the Holy Grail, I thought. Yet struggle towards it we must.

Also there was much poverty and lack of employment caused by three dire bad harvests we had endured, and our trade was suffering cruelly from our debased coinage. Our money had been devalued by Duke Northumberland in my brother's reign and our coins were worth less than some of my nobles' buttons. Besides all these urgencies, there was a peace-treaty between France, Spain and England coming to fruition and even now being talked over at Câteau-Cambresis. At the same time, like an ever-growing grey cloud upon an already restless horizon, lay the unpleasant and threatening fact that Henri II of France had quartered the Royal Arms of England upon those of his son and daughter-in-law. This daughter-in-law of the French King was Marie, Queen of Scotland, great-niece to my father Henry VIII, through his older sister, Margaret Tudor. The French monarch's action was little short of an open insult to England and me.

'Ha, I knew it!' I cried angrily. 'There lies the danger, my Lords, mark you my words. Marie Stuart thinks of herself as rightful Queen of this land. This being so, France will reach out, through her, for England.'

'The lady is but young yet,' said Lord Arundel. 'But fifteen years and with no knowledge of foreign affairs.'

'Young ones grow older,' I retorted, 'and she is fervent Catholic withal. She must be watched closely, I think.'

'Her Grace is right,' acquiesced Cecil. 'Fear not, Madam, she is under surveillance but knows it not.'

I flashed him a smile. 'So be it then. Now, what of the coinage, good sirs? I have been considering this, and it seems to me 'twould be best to call in all cut and mutilated coins and issue new monies of the old sterling standard. 'Tis a strong measure, I know, but desperate cases need desperate remedies, do you not agree?'

They agreed, praising my acumen, discussing ways and means. I enjoyed every minute of those meetings, discovering in myself a true aptitude for governmental politics. Experience I lacked, but time would cure that, and I had Cecil to guide me. In him no ruler could do better. My England, which had been torn and shaken well-nigh to pieces, would be gathered up and made whole by my hand and mine alone, for my Council and ministers, be they never so wise, could do naught without me and my signature. And ·

that signature was not to be had for the asking. Nay, I would hear all and consider all before my hand so much as moved towards my pen. I would have none to deputise for me, or attempt to take the reins of rulership from my fingers. We had known enough of that. Things would be different now.

At this time there returned to Court, from Ireland, good Sir Henry Sidney whence he had been sent by my sister Mary to act as Vice Treasurer and Governor of the Royal Revenues. With him he brought his wife, my dearest Mary Dudley, sister to Rob and friend of my childhood. I had seen neither of them since their marriage over seven years agone and my heart beat high with emotion as they made obeisance before me. Before they were fairly upright, I had pounced forward all muddled 'twixt tears and laughter, and caught them in my arms.

'Now, by the Lord, it is good to see you again, my dears! How fare you? Right well, by your looks! Come, be seated — here are stools and cushions — I want no ceremony with you, my dear friends!'

'Oh Bess, 'tis like a dream, I swear,' said Mary at last. 'I vow I can scarce believe that you, our wild red-head, are verily Queen.'

'And liking it well, I'll warrant,' smiled

Sir Henry. 'You wear the mantle bravely, Madam.'

'Well, it was God's doing, not mine,' I answered. 'The people willed it so, moreover. They truly want me, Harry.'

'As does Rob, it seems,' giggled Mary, her eyes twinkling archly.

'So, so, so!' I laughed. 'He was ever my champion, was he not? Now, will you both stay with me for a while? I would wish you nigh me at my Coronation.'

My Coronation. Ay, that was upon everyone's lips. There was endless discussion as to the state and manner of it. For myself, I wished it to take place on a propitious date, for I would have all auguries to be with me in the hard course I had to run. I was having my hair dressed for the evening, and talking of the matter, when Kat threw down the comb with a cry of triumph.

'I have it! Let us ask Blanche Parry, sweeting! She is Welsh, and if she hath no powers of divination herself, she will know someone who has. How say you to that, my Queen?'

'I say 'tis a good notion. Have her brought to me. And now, Mrs. Katherine Ashley, your Queen says to finish the tiring of her hair, for she refuses to appear in the guise of a gardener's broom!'

38

Laughing, she snatched up the comb and proceeded with my toilet.

The next day we took barge for White Hall amidst great rejoicing and merriment. Blanche came to me there. 'Indeed, I can help you, Madam, my pet,' she assured me. 'Hast forgot my clever cousin, John Dee?'

'Oh, by my faith! He who cast my horoscope and was prisoned for it some years agone?'

'The very same. He foretold your Queenship and straight to gaol went he.'

'Did he not try to persuade my sister to found a Commission for Historical Manuscripts, and is he not well thought of as a mathematician?'

'Ay indeed, my love, and more besides. He is geographer, astronomer, and he is perfecting a way of shortening words into symbols for speedier writing.'

'A very Daniel of wisdom! Well, he must do this task for me of choosing my Coronation Day. Where does this paragon dwell, Blanche? I will send to him.'

'He lives at Mortlake, dearest, and I know will be delighted to undertake your charge.'

'Well, I hope he will choose aright then. I need all the good omens I may get.'

When she had gone, I paced up and down the small parlour, ever and anon leaning upon the projecting, forward-arched, old-fashioned chimney-piece, gazing down into the flames flickering upon the hearth, watching their fitful, ruddy light upon the dull yellow velvet of my gown, changing it to orange, to copper, to shadowed gold. The oak-panelled room grew darker and I smiled to myself at its warmth and cosiness. Here was stability and safety. No more creeping spies, no lurking danger ever ready to strike and cut me down before my rightful flowering. I strode to the door, flinging it wide and shouting for Robert Dudley. He came, all in a flurry, looking ready to devour me with passion then and there.

'Nay Rob!' I protested, struggling laughing from his eager embrace. ' 'Tis not for a secret assignation that I want thee, but for a private mission.' He would not be so summarily denied, so I sat upon his knee by the fire while we kissed and petted. 'I want you to go to Mortlake for me,' I managed to say at last, holding my mouth away from his. 'Rob, Rob, I shall call for Katey Knollys an you do not stop. Did'st hear me? To Mortlake with you, I say!'

'Oh, curse it, what is at Mortlake that is of such desperate import?'

'A man — ' I began, and was instantly cut short.

'What man? Who is it? Why do you want him? And why must I go to this fellow?'

'Sweet Jesu, will you cease your tantrums? 'Tis Dr. John Dee, he who casts horoscopes. I want you to go to him and ask him to find a propitious day for my Coronation.'

'Oh lord, is that all? I thought — '

'I know what you thought, and you are a foolish hothead. Nay,' as he began to protest, 'tomorrow will *not* do. I want you to go now and lose no time over it. Evening is coming on and you may therefore go unnoticed and without fuss.'

'A kiss then, or I am your first rebel!'

I kissed him thoroughly and more than once, to our great pleasure, and off he ran, singing, to do my bidding.

Within the week Dr. Dee was at the gates of White Hall desiring to speak with his Sovereign. I had him brought to me and found him a personable fellow some years older than myself. I gave him my hand to kiss. 'Well, man, well?' I cried eagerly. 'You have a date?'

'I have, your Grace, and I trust it will meet with your approval. It is the fifteenth of January.'

'January! By the stars, 'tis a cold, dark month; raw, windy and with snow too, mayhap. You are certain of this?'

'Full certain, Majesty. 'Tis a day of wondrous promise and augurs naught but good.'

'Have you your calculations with you, Dr. Dee?' He bowed in assent, producing some rolls of parchment from a blue velvet bag carried on a band from his shoulder. 'Show them. I would see these workings and have them explained to me.'

He spread the papers out upon the table and we bent over them. It was of such interest that I kept him a full hour. 'We must begin preparations apace, John Dee,' I said, the interview over, 'for you have left us but little time. I had hoped to have my procession in warmth and sunshine and now 'tis to be in the depths of winter. If your Queen, her Court and all her subjects perish of the rheum, 'tis you will get the blame!'

Alongside the preparations for my Coronation went forward those for Yuletide, which we spent at Richmond. My people were kept right busy with all there was to do, and sempstresses worked day and night to fit me out with gowns as became one of my august condition. Public money was very hard to come by, so much had been wasted by bad governance during the reigns of my brother and my sister, and all financial affairs woefully mismanaged, but I would

42

have nothing niggard about the Coronation. It would not be seemly, nor wished by those I ruled.

One small shock did I receive amongst all the happiness and excitement. A messenger arrived at the palace with the news that a waxen image of me had been picked up in Lincoln's Inn Fields upon the yesterday. It was hideous, but there was a crown upon its head and piercing the breast were three brass pins.

'So!' I said, viewing this small and ugly image. 'Not all my subjects wish me well, it seems. Send for Dr. Dee and bring him here at once. I will brook no delay, and so tell him.'

'Ay, Majesty, 'tis done, never fear. Dr. Dee has seen the Privy Councillors and even now is on his way to you,' answered the messenger from where he knelt before me. 'I was told to make all speed and have outdistanced him upon the way.'

'Well, well, I will wait for him then. I would hear his words from his own lips.'

It was not long before he arrived, in a sad pelter from his hurry. 'Take a cup of wine, John Dee,' I commanded, 'and tell me what you think of this.' I held out my hand, upon the palm of which lay the little doll.

'Ah, I would your Grace had not set eyes

upon the nasty thing. Most distressing. But fear not, dear Lady, 'tis of no import. There are always those who would be contentious and dissatisfied were they in Heaven itself. I do assure you, by all I believe and trust in, that your reign should be long, great and glorious.'

Thus reassured, I put dull care behind me and gave my thoughts to Yule and merriment. Merry Yule it was that year, and gaily did we keep its twelve days. We had masques and mumming, with Rob elected as Lord of Misrule and I as Queen of Beauty. He and I led the revels right joyously and I danced with scarce a pause as the gentlemen, both young and old, strove for my hand in the wild galops and stately pavanes.

In my old mind's eye I see the leaping flames of the great logs, the bright wavering light of the torches in their sconces around the stone walls of the Great Hall, the glow of many waxen candles lighting the smoky air and twinkling in the small coloured panes that filled the huge windows, so that they flashed red, blue and green like enormous jewels. I hear the heavy thump and tap of tabor and drum, the brisk twangling of clavichords, the shrill piping of oboe and flute as we dance The Spanish Lady, Nobody's Jig, Dusty My Dear and the slow

Lady Carey's Dompe. I recall that I wore a robe of silver tissue over a gown of cloth of silver decorated with pearls in clusters shaped like stars and moons. I had my hair dressed all over in curls, a crown of silver and diamonds upon it, and well indeed I looked. My costume caught all the light, as I had intended, so that I stood out from the multitude jigging and hopping around me as 'The Lady Moon in a dark sky,' or so many gentlemen said, and not such young gents, neither. To speak truth, all seemed besotted by me, and I liked it much. Liked it? Nay, I soaked it up like so much old linen, like dry sand. I bathed in it, revelled in it, breathed it in as I would breathe the sweet airs of Heaven.

And it was not only the gentlemen, mark you, 'twas the ladies also. They truly admired me and did their best to imitate my looks and everything I did, in all honesty and love. Ever have I been able to see behind the words and actions of those who would flatter me, and there was no flattery here. I was respected, revered, admired, and best of all, I was loved. A Golden Age is dawning, they said and Elizabeth is its leader, taking us to peace, happiness and prosperity. I had every intention of so doing, and 'fore God I have kept my word.

Dear Rob was in silver too, striped with scarlet, and wearing a most dashing new-fangled short cloak of scarlet tissue lined with panes of silver and scarlet. On his dark head he wore the antlers of the Lord of Misrule, all painted silver and hung with coloured baubles. Of course, we made a scandal at once, for we danced full many a measure with one another, each gazing fondly into the other's eyes and kissing whenever we drew near. For the twelve days of Christmas did we play so, loving and laughing, yet 'twas all harmless and no wrong done, save in our hearts. But there was gossip, oh ay, there was whispering and yammering and tittering in corners; there were censorious looks, ill-disguised, from the elders and excited glances from the young ones. Let them look, let them glance, let them talk scandal! I laughed to myself in glee. I cared not, for I was the power above all and I could stop the whisperings whenever I wished. Besides, I had no intention of truly tarnishing my reputation, or losing the respect of my admirers, although I slid near it once, over the matter of Rob's wife. But that came later.

Just now, thoughts of the Coronation filled all heads, following, as it did, but a bare seven days after Twelfth Night, thus claiming all our attention. Like a dream it all seemed then, each day running into another, slipping by faster and faster, like a silken skein sliding through lax fingers.

'But know ye this,' I said, downright, to Kat, 'no more curls in my hair for the crowning. I will have it plain and flowing. I want no drooping, untwisting hanks falling and slipping about my ears as I had at Yuletide. Then it mattered not, 'twas all fun and jollity amongst ourselves. This is for England and the world.'

★ ★ ★

I think of the fifteenth of January as my wedding day, for I never had another. During that day I was wedded to England by Church and State, by heart and soul, as fastly as ever wife to husband. 'Twas a love that has never died and never will while I live. England is my husband and England's people my children. I love them with a mother's love and they know it well, each and every one. 'Tis a holy thing, beyond flesh and body, rising into the realms of the spirit where are forged chains so fragile as dreams yet stronger than any worldly iron or steel. I know in my deepest being that Almighty God intended me for this high place. He gave me the power of mind, the ability, the strength of will. He chose my parents well, as I now see plain. I am of no half-blood, not I. Mere English I am, and most proud to be. Royal through my great father, and of the people through my brilliant, fascinating mother, who, though her birth was noble, had a Lord Mayor of London and a Cit for a forbear. Truly did my parents bequeath me their charm and hardihood. A cruel childhood and youth did I suffer and the flames of that suffering tempered me fine, so that when the time came I was full ready. And how strangely all the obstacles withered away as the years passed by, gradually bringing me nearer to my destiny. 'Twas not by no man's hand, 'twas by God alone. He had brought this about, and each day I thanked Him for it.

The fifteenth of January was a Sunday, and upon the Thursday before that I had returned to the Tower so that I could make my Recognition Procession from end to end of London, and to the western suburbs beyond, upon my way. This procession was to take place one day before the crowning, so that all folk possible could gain a chance to see me and describe me to those who could not. I would lie the night at White Hall to be ready for the Coronation on the morrow.

It was all arranged very precisely, so that everyone knew his place and what to do.

While at the Tower I took a bath. That bath, why, I had to assert my royal Majesty and shout as loudly as ever my father had done to get my way. It caused a furore worse than the Protestant rebellion in my sister's day! It was winter, I would die of the cold, I would get a fever, be chilled, fall sick of the grippe, the sweat, the plague, and the Lord knew what else. After all, it was not so passing strange that I should wish a bath. All my life long I have taken a bath every month, whether I need it no, and for my crowning I decided that I surely did need it, to be clean before my God.

At length my bidding was done, albeit with gloomy mutterings and dire head-shakings. The tall, lead-lined wooden tub was hauled up the stairs to my chamber and filled with hot water from jugs and pails. Then sweet herbs were sprinkled in, together with lavender and the dried flowers of my favourite violet, so that the steam rose fragrant and inviting. Climbing upon a stool, I stepped into the tub assisted by Kat, Mary Sidney and Katey Knollys.

'More hot water!' I shouted. 'And quickly, before this that I am in grows cold!'

Soon I was up to my armpits and right

good it was, most soothing and merry. I cleansed myself with oil and rosewater and wiped myself with some lace-trimmed cloths of linen which had belonged to my sister. I enjoyed it well, despite the moanings of those about me. It did me good, too, for I slept well and calmly, although Kat was desperate certain that I should get the vapours for my rashness.

In high excitement and anticipation, I rose early the next morn, for the din in the streets would let no one rest, shut the casements and pull the curtains as we would. I found I could eat scarce a morsel, which put Kat into a fine taking and the cook into a pother, but 'twas useless. I swallowed a little wine and a sucket or two, but naught else. At noon Kat and my ladies began to attire me in my gown, which was of cloth-of-gold patterned over with Tudor roses woven into the cloth. Over it I wore a mantle of the same, trimmed and lined with ermine, and over that a small capelet of ermine.

'And a good thing too,' fussed Kat. 'You would die of cold else, ne'er mind John Dee and his prophecies!'

Because of the cold, the body of this gown had been made up to my neck and the strings of my chemise pulled close so that it finished in frills of white lawn which framed my face.

50

Mighty unusual and delicate it looked over all the golden splendour. 'At least my neck will be warm,' I laughed. 'No scarves today, eh Kat? This little ruff should do its work well, I'll warrant.'

'As to that, we shall see,' said Kat grimly. ' 'Tis my belief that all will end with you sick a-bed. I know you.'

'O Heaven, what a doleful misery is my First Lady of the Bedchamber!' I groaned, turning up mine eyes so that all laughed, and Kat too. 'I am near dead with excitement, and here is talk of gloom and sickness. Kat, my love, do not hold down my spirits on this wondrous day. Feel it with me!' I cried. 'I pray all of you, feel it with me!' Jumping to my feet, I overset a jewel-box, a pin-tray and a tiring woman holding ready my slippers, and all was confusion, with me in the centre of it, weeping and laughing together. They calmed me at last and fell to brushing my hair, which was very soothing.

'It shines brighter than your robe, dear Bess,' said my cousin Katey. 'Let us place the golden circlet upon it and you will be ready!'

One young lady who had been hanging from a window, pulled herself in on a sharp command from Kat, to report animatedly that the streets were packed with people from end to end and that the sun shone brilliant from a clear, blue sky.

'You will catch light from its rays and put the sun itself to shame as you look today, my own darling,' cried Kat, seizing me and kissing me upon both cheeks, her eyes full of proud tears. 'Come, it is time. Elizabeth of England, your country awaits you!'

This almost overpowered me and my eyes had to be mopped with a kerchief, but once I stepped forth from my chamber all desire to weep left me. I passed through lines of lords and ladies, all bowing low and curtseying deep like unto the waves of the sea, past my kneeling maids and servants, out into the cold sunshine and down the stone steps to where my chariot of crimson velvet awaited me in the courtyard.

Immediately, four knights came forward to escort me, two to walk at each side of the chariot and to hold up a canopy of crimson fringed with gold over me as I rode. One of these knights was mine own half-brother, Sir John Perrot, a natural son of my father. I had chosen him especially, for he was of my blood and as like my father as his portrait, though shorter, and I had a fondness for him.

'Ho, John!' I called. 'Help me into this chariot and take care not to drop the canopy as we go. We Tudors must stick together, must we not?' He fell to his knees, mumbling emotionally, and I laughed aloud. 'Nay, brother, 'tis your arm I desire, not your knees at this moment. Come, help me up!'

He did so, smiling and brushing his eyes, and as soon as I was seated the procession moved off, with a great retinue going before me, led by trumpeters and heralds in coat-armour, followed by nobles, barons and gentlemen. Behind me rode a large crowd of ladies all in crimson velvet, even to the trappings of their horses, red being the colour of nobility. We clattered over the drawbridge and into the City of London at two o'clock of the afternoon. 'Twas wild and deafening uproar and every face crazy-happy. I had known somewhat of crownings and remembered my sister's very well. I had thought it the summit of excitement, ardour, clangour and uproar, but I swear by God and His angels that my crowning was more than one could dream of or imagine. It was a fantasy past belief had it not been wholly real. All along the way, carpets hung from windows, rich stuffs stretched from house to house fluttered athwart the streets, bells rang, cannon boomed, and firecrackers were let off down every side alley. There were pageants and shows by the score, with children reciting their meaning in rhyme. At Eastchepe, at the church of St. Andrew Hubert, the shouts were so loud that the voice of one small declaiming maiden was quite drowned. I halted my chariot and sent to ask for silence that I might hear the child's words, then listened to the little piping voice with much enjoyment, blowing her a kiss for her pains. After this, the yells were louder than ever. Many wept, dear souls, pressing up close to my carriage with prayers and cries of tenderness and love. I answered them all as lovingly, stretching out my hands as if to embrace them, as I was borne slowly by.

There were some wondrous scenes and pageants made and devised by my Master of the Revels, Sir Tom Cawarden. I halted at each one in very amaze at their beauty and ingenuity. One, at Gracious Street, I remember particularly, for my mother was represented in it, her wedding ring well gilded and bejewelled, this effigy all painted in lifelike hues and set beside one of my father. I was delighted at this and would have stayed longer if it had been possible. Closer and closer pressed the shouting, excited throng, ofttimes one of whom would catch at the side of my chariot to speak to me. Whenever this happened, I would stop and exchange words with him or her, for were these people not mine own? I could feel the love pouring out from them to me as if it were a living thing and they felt my love flowing back and entwining about their hearts. 'Twas extraordinary and miraculous and has never ceased to be so, for I am as well-loved now as I was on that day.

As we came to St. Paul's, a humble countrywoman pushed forward waving a branch of rosemary. I signed to halt. 'Take it your Grace!' she cried. ' 'Tis for you. I have brought it especially for you from Kentish garden lands.'

'Rosemary is for remembrance, is it not?' I smiled.

'Ay, to remember this day, all of us who love you and me who gives this branch to you.'

'I will indeed,' I answered. 'I shall never forget. I shall keep this branch, and here — ' I snapped off a side-branch and returned it to her, 'you keep this in memory of me.'

All cried out and cheered at this as if at some holy utterance. But I kept the branch. 'Twas in my chariot when I reached White Hall. Dry, brown and crumbling now, I have it still . . .

At Paul's Cross the City merchants came out attired in their liveries and gave me a heavy purse containing one thousand mint-new ryals in pure gold, with a long and loyal speech bravely roared out above the din. Some of the coins I threw among the crowd as largesse, but the rest, for prudence, I kept. I needed it most sorely and the merchants could afford to part with it, for at that time they were richer than I.

It was blue dusk before we reached White Hall and my chariot rumbled through the Holbein Gate, the great doors creaking shut behind me. We had proceeded at naught more than a foot-pace for three clamorous, tumultuous miles, and all were exhausted to dropping point save myself. I was lifted to the height of dizzy excitement, almost as if I were drugged or drunken. I could have swum the Thames and felt it not, jumped from the spire of St. Paul's and flown, danced from Westminster to Nonsuch without tiring, or so I felt. I could not keep still, but had my musicians to play merry measures while I tripped it up and down the Long Gallery, laughing and singing alone, for all were too weary for any to bear me company.

At last Kat came to me, a cup in her hand and an expression of would-be sternness on her dear face. 'Come, your Majesty,' she said, 'enough of this. You must a-bed, or your looks will suffer tomorrow.'

56

I twirled upon my toes, head aback, hair flying, arms outflung. 'Oh, Kat, Kat, who can think of bed or sleep? Was it not wonderful? 'Tis like a dream. I am not tired — I could dance and sing all night! What have you in the cup, Madam Mumpsyface?'

' 'Tis a warm posset, my lamb. We must think of the morrow. You would not wish to drop asleep, would you, as the crown is placed upon your head?'

I giggled at the thought, then sobered swiftly. 'Was the crown altered to fit me as I instructed? Was it done? I would not be bowed under its weight and given headaches by it as was sister Mary. I wish it to sit lightly upon my brow as a pleasure, not a pain.'

'Oh ay, 'tis done, fear not. Now, drink this, send away your players and come along, my love. If you are not tired, I am, your ladies are, and everyone else. They must feel well tomorrow also.'

'So be it then, my Lady Fusspot, give me the cup. I will be meek before you. Ugh! What is this that you have given me? 'Tis a sleeping draught, is it not? Oh, crafty Kat, to trick me so. Away with you, good fellows!' I cried to the musicians. 'Your Queen must sleep well before her crowning. And so to our rest,' said I, 'but I warn you, Kat, I shall not sleep a wink.'

But I did, and like a very log, to the relief of all, I daresay.

★ ★ ★

There had been a to-do over the actual moment of my crowning. It was bound to have been so, for I, with the Privy Council at my back, had forbidden any public preaching, for the nonce, and had ruled that services should be read in English so that all could understand. I had announced no definite religious policy, but the Catholic bishops of my sister's reign were grievously upset at my very being, it seemed, and none could be found who would consent to set the crown upon my head! This caused me to veer 'twixt laughter and fury, although 'twas understandable enough. Yet someone had to be found. Undoubted Queen was I, and must be crowned by some holy man of standing. Such a ludicrous situation must be resolved, I shouted, exasperated at the idiocy of the business, and at length it was. Bishop Oglethorpe of Carlisle agreed, against all his tenets, to forswear himself and crown me according to Catholic rites, heretic though he considered me. Such violence did he do his principles by this surrender, that he died shortly after, poor man — of a broken heart, some said, as some will always say. But what would you? A Queen must be crowned!

Well, the day was cold, but fine and bright. A good omen, said one and all, rushing hither and thither about their tasks. A good omen, smiled my ladies and tirewomen, robing me in a high-necked crimson velvet gown. My sleeves, also of crimson velvet and cuffed with ermine, were tied on with great care, then my little ruffled chemise was drawn up about my neck. After that, the stomacher of my gown was laced up the back and pulled down in front to fit well. Over all went a crimson velvet mantle with a long train, and over that I had the small ermine capelet I had worn the day before. Upon my head was set a most stylish little crimson velvet cap which suited me admirably, as my mirror and my ladies assured me.

From White Hall to Westminster Abbey had been spread a long carpet, all of purple, for me to walk upon, and brave it looked against my crimson. My Lord of Shrewsbury walked alongside of me and Lord Pembroke the other, each holding my arms as if I were some precious porcelain figure like to break, and the Duchess of Suffolk followed me, bearing my train. As I stepped slowly along

59

through the crowds, I could hear music from the open doors of the Abbey; organ, pipe and drum, rebec, sackbut, harp, shawms and viol, rising intermittently above the roars of cheers and gunfire.

I had come to the great doors, wherein I could see the brilliance of a myriad candles and smell the heady scent of incense, when I became aware of increased commotion behind me. I could not stop, nor turn to see at such a moment, but was told later that the people in the crowd had fallen upon the carpet and cut it all to pieces for keepsakes before any could stay them. Once inside the Abbey, I was conducted to my anointing amidst great shouts of joy from all within. After this ceremony, I went into a side chapel to change my crimson robes for the golden ones I had worn the previous day. I felt strangely withdrawn and bemused as my ladies whispered excitedly about me.

'You may have to discard this velvet, Majesty,' murmured Lady Frances Cobham, Mistress of the Robes, ' 'tis somewhat marked of oil.'

'Ugh!' said I, but low, 'that oil was grease, I tell you, and stank most ill. I was near to retching at the malodour.' They burst into nervous, suppressed giggles at this as they turned me and tied me into this and that.

At last I was ready and stepped out once more into the scented brilliance of the huge church.

I sat upon the Coronation Chair. I, Elizabeth Tudor, sat upon that holy chair where my sister, my brother, my great father and so many sovereigns of this dear land had sat before me. My dream had come true, the moment was now. Against all trials, all obstacles, I was here. '*Laus Deo*,' I murmured, and my heart swelled within me while my head swam with ecstasy and exultation. Someone had my hands, a ring was pushed on to my finger. I stared down at the Coronation Ring upon the fourth finger of my left hand. My marriage ring, wedding me to England. My eyes filled with tears and I closed them tight for a moment, to restrain the drops from falling. If once I began to weep, I felt I should never stop.

Gazing up into the face of Bishop Oglethorpe as he raised the great Crown of St. Edward above my head, I saw that he looked miserable enough for a funeral. This effectively checked my weeping mood, replacing it by one even more dangerous to my composure. I felt joyous, excited, furious and defiant all at the once. I could scarce contain myself, but the lessons of control, learnt early in my life, stood me in good stead and I remained quiet, even rapt. When I felt the full weight of the crown upon my brow and listened to the echoing roars of '*Vivat Regina Elizabeta!*' a great calm descended upon me and all warring emotions faded away. I felt as one far removed upon a pinnacle or a mountain top, near to Heaven, near to God.

So I was crowned again with the Crown of State and then with the crown that had been made for my dear brother at his crowning, and since altered to fit me. 'Twas a beautiful wreath of diamonds and pearls with hoops of pearl, in front of which was the great glowing jewel called the Black Prince's Ruby, surmounted by a large sapphire. Rising from the chair as one in a dream, I passed through the Abbey for my presentation to the people of the realm.

As the doors drew open, the trumpets sounded, the organ burst forth a-pealing, pipes shrilled, drums chattered, and all the bells of London rang amain. 'As if the world were coming to an end!' gasped the amazed Venetian Ambassador.

Nay, for my world was just beginning . . .

And after that, there was a banquet in Westminster Hall and I there, dressed in violet velvet with silver tissue and pearls. It was three hours after noonday when I washed my hands in the silver bowl and took my seat at the table upon a dais under the great window. Below the dais ranged four tables with two hundred persons seated at each one, and around the walls stood the servers all clad in scarlet. Mine uncle, Lord William Howard, stood at one side of me and good Tom Radcliffe, Earl of Sussex, at the other, ready to serve me with their own hands, although I ate but little, being too overwrought. And all about the hall rode my Lords of Arundel and Norfolk, each a-horseback, to see that all went as planned, for they had charge of the banquet. I spoke but little to those around me, being too overcome by the awe and majesty of my crowning, but I did address the Lords in a few heartfelt words of thanks for their work on my behalf, for the Coronation and all its goodly show within and without. Raising my glass, I drank to them, and as I did so, all the Lords took off their coronets and there was a great fanfare of trumpets. Yet it all went on outside me, for I was far away, floating high above, suspended, in a mystic aura of holiness and Queenship.

We did not reach our beds until after one o'clock of the next morning. There had been a joust arranged for that day, but I slept all through, waking at last with a raging sore throat and a head that ached as if screwed into an iron band. A mighty rheum had I, even as Kat had foretold, and loud and dismal were my sneezes, sniffs and coughings.

'I told you so! I told you so!' she fretted. 'A se'ennight abed for you, my Queen, no matter what Your Majesty may say to the contrary!'

I said naught whatever to the contrary, being only too glad to lie cocooned in blankets behind the bed-curtains, for I was exhausted as well as enrheumed. For several days I lay, too drained of emotion to care what took place around me. The Coronation ceremony had wrought upon me like a spell. I was never quite the same after. Mayhap I had been brushed by the mantle of God.

2

THRONES, DOMINATIONS AND POWERS

1559 – 1560

It had been arranged for me to open
Parliament on the twenty-third of January,
but because of my indisposition, this had
been delayed for two days. The welcome
I had from the people in the streets soon
brought the colour back to my pale cheeks. I
waved and smiled, happy to see them, calling
my thanks for their loyalty.

At the door of Parliament House I was
met by the Abbot of Westminster, with his
monks holding candles and torches. This was
too Popish-seeming for me to countenance,
and to show my feelings, I cried aloud, so
that all could hear: 'Away with those torches,
Master Abbot, we see very well!' They fell
back, disconcerted, and I passed within. ' 'Tis
but ten o'clock of the morn,' I said clearly.
'We need no lights at this hour.'

All understood this perfectly well, as I had
meant them to do. Although I had been
crowned according to Catholic rites, I had

no desire to be thought to favour the old religion. I had to steer a middle course, for all England had endured enough of fanatical religious beliefs. I wished to heal and build, not to destroy. I smile, now, to myself as I call to mind the cheers that greeted me as I entered the House. The members looked truly glad to see me and I was eager to begin work as a young horse fretting in the lists at a tourney.

Sir Nick Bacon, Cecil's fat brother-in-law, whom I had created Lord Keeper of the Great Seal, welcomed me in a most rousing speech. 'How fortunate are we,' he cried, 'to have a princess to whom no wordly thing is so dear as the hearty love and goodwill of her subjects!'

A great shout came then, with tears on many cheeks. It is the truth; though to see me now, toothless and wrinkled, white-haired under my wig, and with a rheum, few would believe it. 'Twas a strange thing, the feeling I inspired and continued so to do. It was as if I were some human lodestone that attracted all to me, whether I would or no. In my early days, to restrain my pride, I would tell myself that it was caused through relief after the troubles of my brother's and sister's reigns, but the older I grew, the longer I ruled, the stronger wrought the magic. It is not gone, even yet, although my days are now numbered to but a few, my rheumatism is bothersome and my cold refuses to leave me . . .

Much work we did that day in Parliament, for a religious policy had to be settled and made final. Two Acts we passed. One was that of Supremacy, which applied to posts temporal and spiritual under the Crown, making them subject to me as Queen and Supreme Governor of the Church. For men holding such posts, to attack my religious policies was treason, therefore, but only to be penalised at the third offence, for I wished to show moderation as well as firmness.

The Act of Uniformity I worked out myself. It has been called a masterpiece of compromise, for 'twas designed to cause no ill-feeling to either Catholic or Protestant unless one faction or the other was determined to make trouble. 'I wish to open no windows into men's souls,' I said, 'nor let it be said that *our* reformation tendeth to cruelty.'

It was a difficult position that I had to maintain, for near half my realm was Catholic, as was most of Europe, and Philip of Spain, too, with all his wide dominions. My English Catholics were almost all ready to be loyal to me, yet they owed fealty to the

Pope also. So I had to guide my policy as a pilot guides his boat through rocky straits in foggy weather, ever conscious of shoals and sandbanks, rocks and deeps. Then, as we talked and discussed, there came forward my own personal rock, against which my assurance and determination foundered. It was the subject of my marriage. Hastily I put these good men off with fair words and half-promises, telling them that I would attend to the matter later.

They left me but twelve days to myself before taking it up again. I was walking amongst my ladies and gentlemen, Rob at my side, in the Great Gallery at White Hall, discussing alterations to the building and the necessary moving of furniture and hangings, with much talk and laughter. Outside, the weather was wild and wet, the river blown into grey billows by gusts of wind. We could descry trees on the south bank bent near double in the gale. But my ministers cared naught for the weather, for here came a Parliamentary deputation to wait upon me concerning a 'grievous, vexed and worrisome subject,' or so said the spokesman. So, waving back my companions, I sat upon my chair at the long table with these good fellows, each one red-nosed and blown by the wind.

' 'Tis of the matter of your marriage, Majesty.'

God save us, that again, I thought in exasperation. Leaning my elbows upon the polished oaken tabletop, I surveyed the earnest faces surrounding me. 'As to that,' I said smoothly, 'I will act as God directs me.'

'But dearest Majesty, the Succession — ?'

'As to that,' I murmured, 'God may direct me not to marry.'

Never have I seen eyes open so swiftly in such alarm and dismay. Jaws hanging, the deputation stared at me as if I had grown two heads before their very faces. Agape, they gazed at one another and then back at me. 'Not to marry? Not to *marry*! Nay, Majesty, all Sovereigns must marry!'

I raised my brows thoughtfully as one who considers a problem. 'Then no doubt God will provide for the Succession in His own way,' I said equably. 'See you here,' and I drew from one long, white finger my Coronation Ring and held it up before them, 'I am already bound to a husband, which is the Kingdom of England,' I stated. 'As for my own wishes, gentlemen, it will be enough if it is writ on a marble stone when I am gone: '*This Queen, having reigned such a time, lived and died a virgin.*' '

Make what you will of that, thought I, as they apologised for importuning me and went away. But I knew I had not heard the last of that question. Nor had I. It was to plague me for years. I did not wish to marry, nor ever had. I had said it oft enough and none would believe me. I would have no man, nor any person to take one jot of power from me. I could be subject to no husband, 'twas not in my nature. Moreover, I did not want to share the love of my people with another. I was their Daystar, their All in All, their Own Elizabeth. They had said it, they had writ it, called it out after me. It was so, and so it should stay.

Seated alone at the table, head on hand, I pondered this. I was the greatest marriage catch in Europe. I knew it well, and my availability could be of immense use to me in foreign affairs. If I married, I would lose my bargaining power, which, as I saw it, was worth more than the mightiest of alliances. And, hated thought, would not a husband wish to have a say in my policies, both at home and abroad? Ah, never, never! Might I not become pregnant, and thus unwell and unable to take my place at Council meetings? Worse yet, might not He, the Husband, take that place? Anathema, unthinkable! No and no and no. Besides — and a chill ran through

70

me — I feared, I feared . . . *blood* . . . *death . . . the grave . . .*

Springing to my feet, I called for lights, music, dancing, quick, quick, enough of heavy thought and doleful dumps, let us dance, let us sing, let us be merry, for Youth is precious and a new age dawns! So we danced, all the company and Rob and I. I had no other for partner, nor wished it; the very touch of his hand was flame to me, and my flame was lit in his hot, black eyes. So brave and jaunty did he step it, how beautiful he looked as he pranced and turned, cloak a-swing, hand on hip. His legs were so long and well-shaped for a man, his shoulders so broad, his belly so flat. Beautiful. It was not only I who thought so, neither; all the ladies were mad for him, but he had eyes only for me. Many there were who thought that he made up to me because I was Queen and for what I could give him. Well, and so he may have, a little, but he desired me for myself and always had. I was never a self-deceiver and could ever tell truth from counterfeit, it was a knack born in me. Nay, he loved me and I knew it. We could not keep our eyes from one another, nor our hands from patting and our lips from kissing if near enough. His height, his princely walk, the graceful carriage of his handsome head — ah

Rob, my darling, such a man as you were! And I was of your kind, it was as simple as that. We had no thought of discretion, nay, rather we gloried in our love and desire and scorned to hide it. Such gossip as we caused, he and I! It roared about our ears and we cared not. I was in love with him and never let him leave me, went the rumour, first whispered, then chattered, then spoke of aloud. Ay, for once rumour was right. Indeed I wished him always at my side and made no secret of it. Another morsel of gossip was that I refused to marry because I could not have Rob as a husband, he having a wife already, and no other man would do for me.

Kat twittered about it every day. ' 'Twill lessen your popularity; 'tis not meet for a lady to caress a man in public — still less a married man. 'Tis not right for a Queen to behave so,' and on and on in the same strain.

'Nay,' I retorted one day, 'who is anyone to say what is meet for me to do? I am the Queen. If I wish to love Lord Robert, I shall!'

'What!' she shrieked, sitting down plump on a stool. 'Have you bedded with him, then? Oh, you are mad, my pet!'

'So are you to bellow such things, Kat.' Guiltily she clapped her hand over her mouth. 'Are not my ladies constantly in my apartments and bedchamber, about their duties, watching me day and night?'

'Ay,' she answered somewhat doubtfully; 'it is indeed so, but I know you could make the chance if you so wished.'

'Hey, well-a-day! If I do, I shall not tell you nor any other.'

'But, my lamb, have you considered? What if you should fall pregnant? Oh, 'tis too awful to contemplate. I do pray you to keep your wits, my darling.'

'Oh, cease your chirruping, Kat. How you do take me up! Of course I have considered. I believe I shall not fall pregnant. I am too afeared, I think, to take the risk.'

Ay, I was afeared, and perhaps it was a good thing, for each time our lovemaking reached a point from which we could not retreat, this fear would spring forth and restrain me from actual coupling. It drove us nigh crazy, and oft did I near succumb when I felt ready to give all and the world well lost, but always at the last moment, even at the act itself, something seemed to happen to my body to close it against my darling. I am sure it was fear that wrought thus upon me. I can see no other reason. The tale that I was not as other women, and other such foolish babble, did indeed reach my ears and caused Rob and me to die a-laughing.

Once I thought I had mischanced, but my monthly courses were very irregular, sometimes missed altogether, and my worry at that time was, luckily, needless. Ridiculous too, I thought then, for if a man be not inside a woman, reasoned I, he could not impregnate her. Yet since I have heard that this need not be so, that a man's seed near enough to a woman's secret parts at a certain time may be enough to result in a child. I have been told lately of two such cases, both well authenticated, although when that perilous certain time for a woman may be, no doctor seems able to tell, so great are the mysteries of Nature.

Rob and I knew naught of such danger, and so did take risks, as I realise now. I thank God they came to nothing, although I would have loved a child, be there another way of getting one. Even if we had married, I doubt my body would have opened to him, even though he forced me. It was something more than myself and my conscious desires, something fashioned in my mind since babyhood and childhood, and wrought stronger by the tragedy of my Lord Admiral whom I had loved and who had died by the axe more than ten years afore. Besides, marriage would have given Rob domination over me and that

I could not concede.

Domination or no, how could I not show sympathy for poor, dear Rob when he complained to me of the strange dampness of the walls in his rooms upon the ground floor? 'Of course he must have others!' I cried. ' 'Tis only right!' How peculiarly apt that I should find a vacant suite immediately adjoining mine own! Kat at once gave tongue.

'So now his lodgings are next and nigh your own! So your ladies watch you day and night, do they? By the Lord, my love, what next?'

'Kat, I will have no more prattle upon this subject. I will have my way in it, and so I tell you. Be silent, my dear, for I will brook no interference. Things are as I wish, and that is enough.'

So she fell silent, looking sad and abashed. Flinging my arms about her, I kissed her heartily. 'Oh my sweet,' she said, 'I love you so dear that mayhap I fret overmuch.'

I laughed, and began wickedly to sing:

'Robin loves me,
'I am his.
'Robin sought me
'For his true love,
'He'll have me.'

As I sang, I danced about the chamber, pirouetting and sinking in a flourishing curtsey before her.

'Ay,' she said glumly. 'Have you, he may well do.'

'Oh, Kitty-Kat, how you do fuss! Like you not this pretty pomander he has given me? See, it hangs at my waist upon this gold chain.' I was all girlish innocence.

'I marked it,' she said tersely. 'Have you given him aught in return?'

'Oh, not what you are thinking! Some good plate in gold only. He is not the only one to whom I give gifts. What of those at New Year to my bishops, to my friends, my household, eh Kat? Much good money they cost me, too!'

★ ★ ★

It was a sweet springtime, that year of 1559, the first of my reign, with much sunshine and clement weather. Upon St. George's Day I went to Baynard's Castle at Blackfriars to sup with my Lord Pembroke. As I stepped into my barge, I looked about me, across the sparkling waters of the Thames, at the bushes and trees all a-bud and greening. I saw the towers of the gatehouse at Lambeth Palace, and the horse-ferry moving slowly across the water, with a horse and two men aboard. One fellow waved to me, bobbing his head respectfully, and I waved back. Once I was seated, the oars plashed us swiftly on our way. Rob and I sat together under the violet silk canopy, hand in hand, laughing and whispering amongst the ladies and gentlemen who accompanied me.

A good and courtly supper we had, and I thought the castle fine; within richly appointed in the modern style, though old-fashioned as to the building. But it had great charm in its very antiquity, with its towers and turrets rising against the sky, an ever-pleasant landmark. After the meal, I took a boat and was rowed up and down the river. The news of my visit to Baynard's had been bruited about and all the good folk were out to watch me. There were upwards of an hundred boats and barges rowing about me, their inmates waving, cheering, throwing flowers and sweetmeats, whilst on the banks were great crowds thronging to look upon me. Some were wetted about the feet and legs, being pushed into the water, willy-nilly. In some boats were musicians blowing trumpets, beating drums and playing the flute. Guns were constantly discharged and squibs hurled into the air as my boat was rowed from place to place. It was delightful to me, and we all kept it up until ten o'clock of the night, when I departed home to White Hall amid happiness, rejoicings and loving cries from my dear people.

I showed myself much abroad, for I loved to do so, and the crowds loved it as much as I. Well did I know that there were those who but waited for me to make a false step and lose the respect and adoration of my subjects. I knew too, that there were many who thought that such a honeymoon could not last, and were never tired of prating examples that proved this dismal theory. But oh, I was young, vital, beautiful and beloved, the weather was fair, summer was near. I was Queen and I had Rob. Happy, happy Elizabeth!

At this time, news came from France that my cousin, Marie Stuart, wedded since a year to the French Dauphin, was sick and like to die. Cecil had it in a letter from Sir John Mason.

'Sir John fears she will not long continue, Madam,' said Cecil, tapping the parchment he held upon the palm of his other hand.

'What, at fifteen?' I cried. 'What is it with her, then?'

'She suffers greatly from strange humours of the body, Madam, swooning, much biliousness and vomiting, pains in the side and chest, pains in the legs and swellings all about her.'

'Is it the nephritis? I have had that, remember, and more than once.'

' 'Tis not known. She suffers vilely from the headache, sore throat and shortness of breath, moreover, and when not white and swooning, talks fast and wildly.'

'Jesu, Cecil! What else says Sir John?'

'He prays God to take her to Him so soon as may please Him,' answered Cecil blandly, eyes cast down.

'Well, then?' I said quietly.

He glanced up, his eyes met mine and held them. I raised my brows, a tiny quiver touched his mouth and was gone. No words were needed; we both felt the same about my cousin Marie. She was a devilish nuisance, for she felt herself to be my heir and spared no pains to show it. More than heir, to say truth. She had been heard to say many times that my throne was hers by right. Indeed, Henry II of France had formally proclaimed her to be Queen of England, Ireland and Scotland, and had caused her to assume the Royal Arms of England as well as her own, when my sister died. Wretched girl, why had she to be born at all? She caused naught but trouble from her birth.

In a way, she did have a certain claim on

my throne, for she was the granddaughter of my father's elder sister, and, according to Catholic belief, my parents were never married. Strict Catholics considered me illegitimate, as well I knew, having been pronounced so, legally, by mine own sister before being received at last into her favour. Yet my father had given in his will that the throne was not to go to a foreigner, and by this, my cousin was debarred from such pretensions. It was a mighty vexing situation. If this illness could but carry her off, it would be a good way out of many forseeable difficulties.

'Is she beautiful, Cecil?' I asked suddenly.

'Ambassador Nick Throckmorton writes that all say she is.'

'Oh, as to that!' I said scornfully. 'Mere courtiers' talk is that. Is it true that her colouring resembles mine?'

'Ay, she hath red hair, white skin and golden eyes like your Majesty. Her hair be of a darker red, though.'

'Tall? Short? Fat? Thin? Tell me.'

'I hear she is very tall — near two yards high.'

'Faith, a maypole!'

'Very slender — '

'Lanky then! Her features?'

'Most regular, they say.'

'Ha! Long-nosed, they mean! 'Tis said of me, and my nose is long, too.'

He smiled. 'Yours is fine aquiline like your great father's.'

'Oh, I know I am no true beauty, no matter what is said, Cecil. Yet how well I love to hear it said! It is music to mine ears, vain creature that I am.'

'You are very woman, dearest Queen; why should you not love to hear such? Moreover, there is something about you that bewitches not only men, but women too. Remember that. It is a gift that few possess, be they never so beautiful.'

Impulsively I seized his hand. 'Dearest Spirit, dear Will, what a comfort are you to me! You know me as none other, save my Kat, and no other man serves me so well. I would have you with me always.'

And so I did. He never left me. Most of his time he abode at Court, despite his great houses, his pleasant wife and his family. Where I went, so went he, my Spirit. When I lost him, I lost part of myself, I swear . . .

Soon after this news of my cousin, I was delighted to learn that our negotiations at Câteau-Cambresis had met with success and that the peace treaty between England, France and Spain had been signed. I could breathe easy now that the danger of war had been removed, and seek to build up my poor country.

In May, Cecil received tidings from Throckmorton that my cousin, having recovered from her previous seizure, was now ill again. 'She is pale and green, short-breathed withal, and it is whispered among them that she cannot live long, so writes Throckmorton,' said Cecil as we paced up and down the Long Gallery.

'She will recover yet again,' said I resignedly. 'She has a great will to live, methinks. My sister had just such until she lost it, then she died. I too have a great will. Mayhap 'tis that which sustains our sickly family. I could wish that my cousins' were not so strong.'

He laughed and took himself off.

At the end of the month an embassy came from France to receive my ratification of the Treaty of Câteau-Cambresis. It was a great occasion; the greatest since my crowning, and I gave a supper in the garden at White Hall, a pretty fancy of mine, and unusual at the time. I ordered the Piazza below the Long Gallery to be hung with gold and silver brocade, the open side to be decorated thick with garlands and wreaths of fresh flowers. Beautiful indeed it looked and smelled. At one end of the Piazza, I had a door made all of roses for me to use at my entrance — 'twas delightful. I call it to mind entire in its fresh beauty and sweet, heady scent.

For this gathering I wore a new gown of pale purple velvet, very soft and rich, and to impress my visitors, I was near covered with jewels, gold and pearls. It would show them that I was no meek mouse, content to hang back and take the words of others for my belief, that I was no mere woman to be overruled. It would also demonstrate that the Queen of England was far from a pauper sovereign of an impoverished Kingdom, but a force that they would come to recognise and reckon with. Again I blessed the jewels left me by my father. Once more they had done me a timely turn. Kat and Mary Sidney said I looked as gaudy as a peacock, but I cared naught for that.

' 'Tis but policy, silly ones!' I cried. 'Our visitors will be impressed as I intend they should, and so carry the tale of my richness and consequence back to their masters.'

I received my guests at six of the clock, greeting them in French, and I saw by their faces that they were struck with admiration for my appearance and my command of their tongue. Giving each of the Ambassadors my hand, I charged them and the company to walk with me in the late afternoon sunshine under the trees in the private orchard while supper was readying. As we strolled under the leafy branches of the apple trees, I told Monseigneur de Montmorenci and Monseigneur de Vielleville of the douleurs I had suffered in my sister's reign, and how I was oft nigh unto being put to death, yet saved from this fate by the love the people of England bore for me.

At seven, the trumpets sounded, and I led the way into supper through the door made of roses, much praised by the Frenchmen for its beauty and originality. In the Piazza, the tables had been set up, upon them an array of drinking cups all in gold and rock crystal, and the Ambassadors exclaimed at them as they glittered in the westering sun. There was quite a press, and some of the ladies whose skirts were very wide, had, perforce, to sit upon the floor, causing much calling and laughter, while the gentlemen waited upon them. It was delightful informal and had the feeling of a country picnic, in spite of all our splendours.

After we had eaten, we repaired to the upper gallery of the Tilt-yard, where there was to be held a mock battle. I thought it a beautiful spectacle, there in the gathering darkness, the rich apparel of the lords and ladies glowing in the light of an infinite number of torches held by the Guard, each one of whom was clad in crimson and gold, stray gleams flashing here and there off a jewel or a brooch like little stars come down to earth.

The contestants were Walter Devereux, Viscount Hereford, dressed all in silver, with twelve gentlemen armed at all pieces, dressed in white against Manners of Rutland, likewise in silver, but with his gentlemen all in blue. For a signal, I struck a bell and cried: 'Allez vous en!' and they closed in combat with much shouting and hollering which my guests enjoyed greatly, urging on the fighters with shouts, arm-wavings and laughter.

After that, we walked about the Long Gallery, where I showed the Frenchmen the special portrait of my brother as a child, made by Holbein. This is a strange work, for, to a person standing before it, it is so ugly and has such a long nose that it scarcely seems human. They puzzled at it for a while, not knowing what to say so as not to offend me at the hideousness of my poor brother. Then I told a page to give them a certain broad tin sheet, three spans long, with a little hole to spy through, and laughed heartily at the change in the expression of each as he stared through in his turn, for there before his eyes was revealed Ned's fine, well-formed countenance instead of the grotesque face seen at first. They thought, as I do, that this is a great work of art.

Then we danced until eleven o'clock and all very merry. When my guests took their departure, I gave them gifts of hounds and horses, and gold and silver plate, also some of the best and richest of my dear brother's suits for the Seigneur de Montmorenci's young brother, a pretty lad much of the same size and age of poor Ned before his death. The suits were beautiful and quite unworn, and the boy was delighted, for they were fit for a king, as indeed he said.

Although all seemed light and glittering as a bauble upon the surface of my Queenship, there were dark and grave considerations beneath, and these much occupied my thoughts, for I was never one to shy away from reality. Queen though I was, my position was fragile in the eyes of the world, for without ceaseless watch and delicate care, my cousin Marie could easily become the focus of Catholic hopes, even as I had been the focus of Protestant hopes in my sister's reign. There could be plot after plot in her name to further the Catholic cause. If this should be the case, and she decided to take a hand herself, she would have the blessing of the Pope in her venture to unseat me and the power of France to aid her.

'Heigh-ho, naught is as easy as it seems,' I observed one morning to Cousin Katey, who was waiting upon me. 'It is by no means all gaiety to be a Queen. 'Tis a grave responsibility, and this question of Scots Marie is very difficult and uneasy.'

'Never mind, dearest,' answered Katey. 'Let us think of merrier things, such as your Progress into Kent. Even now we are almost ready to leave for Greenwich.'

'Ay, so we are indeed!' I cried excitedly, jumping to my feet. 'Hey, Katey, I'll warrant Frances Cobham is in a rare to-do at Cobham Hall! Almost do I feel sorry for her, having to entertain me and all of you who accompany me. But I long to see lovely Kent at this time of the year, and I hear that the gardens of Cobham are notable fine. Has Kat seen to all my gowns and such? 'Tis the Lady Frances's place to do it, but since she is away, Kat has taken on the task.'

'Mistress Ashley is equal to anything, as well you know, Bess,' answered my cousin, laughing. 'Did she not have charge of you from a young one?'

'Saucy bitch that you are!' I grinned. 'I have a good mind to leave you here at Court. Where is the deference due to your Sovereign

Lady? My sister would have had you in the Tower for less!'

★ ★ ★

And so we left for Kent on my first Progress. Down river to Greenwich and Placentia did we go, to the place of my birth and the home of my tiny babyhood. Slipping over the rippling Thames water, we rounded the curve at Deptford, and there lay the long, pink brick waterfront, all turretted and embattled, its many windows twinkling in the sunshine. Dominating all rose the Gatehouse, rising sheer from the river and spanning the footpath, joining the main façade by another tower taller still, of five stories high. My heart beat fast as I disembarked, the trumpeters blowing a fine blast in my welcome. I passed, smiling, through the Gatehouse, across the quadrangle and into my private apartments. From the windows I could see Greenwich Hill surmounted by old Duke Humphrey's Tower, all so sweetly green and covered with wild flowers that I fetched a breath of joy and thanks-giving at the sight. I glanced downward to the Privy Garden where roses bloomed, with purple pansies for company, golden marybuds and those little pink coronation flowers, now called carnations after the modern fashion. Mine now, and all I could see, praise be to God.

There was a great demonstration to mark my visit. I watched the show from the South Gatehouse that spans the road to Woolwich. Upon the Great Lawn this day, men of the militia shot guns and clashed pikes together, running about and shouting in imitation of a fierce battle. I enjoyed it finely, calling my thanks from the window.

We stayed not long at Placentia, leaving betimes for Kent and travelling 'all through the wilds,' as some complained. There are those who would complain at Heaven itself, be they so fortunate as to reach it. Kent was Heaven enough to me in those merry days, as we made our way, laughing and singing, down Watling Street to Eltham Palace, over Shooter's Hill, through Bexley Village and Dartford, all by easy stages to Singlewell, then up the great swell of Shorne Ridge to Shorne Woods atop the rise. Ah, 'twas good to be alive, thought I, with the sunlight filtering through the leaves, the air full of bird-song, Rob riding at my left hand and Cecil at my right. I gave the signal to halt, and looked back. There, obediently drawn up behind me, were my guards, my ladies and gentlemen, my household people, and three hundred baggage carts, each drawn by five or six strong horses. Hey, it was a fine sight, and all for little I, a slender, pale-faced, red-headed chit — a fine sight indeed!

The fair Kentish countryside rose and fell in gentle hills about us, thickly wooded, lush and fertile. I breathed deep of the summer-scented air and allowed my eyes to rove again over the prospect before me. All mine. All mine to care for, to husband, to cherish, to protect and preserve. So would I do while there was breath in my body. Sighing happily, I recalled myself to the present, realising that my messengers must have reached Lady Frances to tell of our arrival. I rose in the saddle, pointing down the lane.

'Forward now, my lords and ladies!' I called. 'On, to Cobham Hall!'

And so we went forward. Poor Frances, what an undertaking she had before her! Soon the Hall was filled to overflowing, but my people had been found places in the village and round about. Such a to-do was there while my baggage carewares, each on their two wooden wheels, bumped into the courtyard, with grooms and servants bawling and running everywhere, Stabling had to be accomplished, and great was the din of horses' hooves clattering upon the cobbles among the shouting of orders from gentlemen and guardsmen as to the bestowal of their mounts. Someone said that there were four hundred horses in all; I am sure there were no less.

Frances was awaiting me in the porch with her lord, looking at once excited and apprehensive. I dismounted, placing my foot into the clasped hands of a kneeling groomsman, and jumped lightly on to the flagstones. Lord Will and Lady Frances at once made deep obeisance and I gave them my hands to kiss.

'Rise, Will; up, my dear Frank, stand no more upon ceremony with me. Right glad am I to see you. God's Body, but you have a pleasant house. I like it well from the outside. Will you show me within?'

Inside, the house was as good as any could have wished. All had been done to study my comfort, and the rooms I had been allotted overlooked the famous gardens which were in their highest beauty. The formal garden lay direct below my window, the parterres a mass of roses whose scent reached me even in my chamber. My room, too, was of the finest. Frances told me that the Hall had been enlarged and rebuilt especially against my coming, and that the Banqueting Hall was so lately thrown up that it was but only just now finished.

After we had dined, we wandered about those beautiful gardens all the afternoon. There were the loveliest walks, some turfed, some sanded, some planted with burnet, wild thyme, water-mint and catmint, to perfume the air when trodden on. There was a small garden made entire of lavender, walled in with high green box hedges, there were shady alleys arched over with the boughs of willow, lime and whitethorn, and a long pleached alley with briars and scarlet runners trained over. Arbours and secluded resting places were everywhere, and then there was the Tree House, a wondrous thing indeed.

It was built in a great lime tree which had been trained so that its branches grew in three flat tiers outwards from the trunk, and upon these tiers planks were laid. The first platform, reached by steps leading up from the ground, was strong enough to hold fifty men or nearabouts, and from thence more steps ran up to two higher tiers; a very marvel and like none I had seen. I resolved upon some such to be tried at Richmond or Nonsuch for my pleasure.

While at Cobham, I rode often abroad to show myself to the Kentish people, to receive their welcome and to hear any troubles and complaints they might have, to settle their disputes if I could. I watched their entertainments that they had got up for me and enjoyed them thoroughly, rustic and simple though they were. Some folk wept their delight to see me, all cheered and sang amain, and many were the pretty, countrified gifts they brought me in their kindness. How could I not love my dear people who themselves loved me so well? When I look back upon that happy time, it seems to be made all of music, sunshine, green leaves, blue skies, roses, sweet scents, bright satins, smiling faces, dancing and laughter; a jewel in my memory.

Only one discordant note was struck, and that was when Cecil came to me with a paper in his hand as I was walking in the gardens. He told me that Henri II of France was feared by all to die, for he had been injured in a tourney, a lance having pierced through his eye to the brain. The news had reached us late, having gone to London first, but Cecil thought we should hear more soon. And so we did, within a day or two. I was sitting upon a turfed seat planted with pennyroyal that gave off a sweet savour, the arbour trees affording a grateful shade. My ladies and gents were all about me and we were laughing at some jest of

Nick Bacon's. Seeing Cecil approaching, I held up my hand for silence.

'Leave us, my dears,' said I. 'Good Sir William has something of import to tell me, so be off with you now.' Motioning Cecil to sit beside me, I turned to him. 'What now, Sir Spirit? No good, I'll warrant from your sober visage.'

'Nay indeed,' he replied. 'The French King is dead of his wound, but he lived a full ten days screaming in agony before expiring on the 10th of July.'

'So now my cousin is Queen of France,' I said. We fell silent for a space, then I went on: 'I trust that her husband dies not young, or she will bring a mountain of troubles upon my head. At least, while she is Queen of France, it will keep her out of my way, whatever her designs upon my throne.'

Cecil wagged his head glumly. 'The new King is very sickly, they say, Madam. 'Tis doubted he will make old bones.'

'Oh Lord,' I sighed. 'Nothing runs smooth for long, does it? Well, let us hope he dies not before my Progress is finished. I do wish to enjoy it with as clear a mind as possible.'

'Let us pray, then, for his long life,' said Cecil, smiling.

'Amen to that,' I answered fervently.

It was a happy Progress, for the weather

stayed fine, even after Cobham. Wherever I rested, my welcome was great and much was made of me, giving happiness to all, although it cost the nobles, my hosts, a mort of money. And why should it not? Most of them had, at that time, far more than I who had been left a depleted Treasury, a debased coinage, a divided country, and as yet a very small personal allowance for one of my rank and state. Besides this, such travellings of mine would keep the nobles aware of my presence, of my guiding hand, and, most important, my knowledge of their personal doings and their wealth.

★ ★ ★

Short of money I may have been, short of suitors for my hand I was not. Word o' God, they came thick and fast by way of their Ambassadors. The Danish Ambassador wore a crimson velvet heart stuck with an arrow upon the breast of his doublet, to show the state of the King his master's heart, for love of me. Then there was the Archduke Charles of Austria sending love-maddened messages.

'Lord!' I said, laughing, to Mary Sidney, 'this one is hot for me whom he has never seen!'

'You jest, I know, my love,' answered Mary, smiling, 'but would it not be better and safer for you to have a husband to guard you?'

'What, are you thinking of that plot at your brother Ambrose's supper party?'

'Indeed I am, dearest. You treat it very lightly. Ambrose was overset for days. A plot to poison you and stab Robert is not to be laughed at, surely?'

'Well, it came to naught, did it not? I dare say there will be many such in years to come. There are always malcontents whom naught can satisfy. Yet, mayhap,' I went on, my eyes twinkling mischievously, 'I might fancy to find safety in marriage with the good Archduke. Tell that to the new Spanish Ambassador, it will keep him happy, no doubt.'

As I had expected, Alvarez de Quadra, Bishop of Aquila, the Ambassador from Spain who had replaced De Feria, soon sought to speak to me. I was leaning out of a casement of the Waterside Gallery, shouting down to Robert who was in a boat upon the river below the windows, when he came bowing and craving speech with me.

'Well, what is it man?' I cried testily, having been interrupted in setting a wager upon Rob to beat another Court gallant in a rowing race.

' 'Tis of the Archduke Charles, Madam,' he answered in his heavy Spanish-English.

'So, and what of him?'

'I hear you might consider him as a husband, *Vuestra Majestad*.'

'To consider is one thing, to take is another, De Quadra.' I began to pace up and down the long room, he beside me. 'I could not marry a man I have never seen!'

'*Yo pienso* — I think — if he be asked here, to London, *Majestad* — '

I ceased my walking and stared at him in mock-amaze. 'What, invite him here to London, to my Court, as if I were hanging out for a man? What immodesty, sir!'

De Quadra lapsed into Spanish. 'But you, as Queen, would be above such censure,' he said hopefully, 'would you not?'

'Oh, as to that I cannot agree, dear Bishop,' I replied, answering him in his own tongue. 'I am incurring censure enough over the person of Lord Robert Dudley. Surely if the Archduke came to London he would hear rumours against my reputation. There are many such rumours, as I know. This being so, might not the Archduke refuse to marry one of seemingly sullied virtue?'

'My dearest Queen, no, no! The Archduke

Charles is a very great gentleman, and moreover, you must remember that I know everything that happens at Court. If there had been aught of truth in these scandals, I would know. Rest assured of that. Shall he visit you?'

'Well, I will think on it,' I said, 'and I will tell you my mind later.'

So De Quadra had a spy system at my Court, had he? I had thought as much, the cunning knave. As for the Archduke Charles, a little uncertainty as to my favours and wishes would keep him sweet, and fearful also to offend me and my country. He could wait. There were other matters to occupy my attention, for my cousin Marie, and Francis her husband, were now crowned King and Queen of France. The new King Francis was threatening to have himself proclaimed King of Scotland, England and Ireland. It were bad enough for Marie to do so, but for Francis it was sheer insolence.

'My God!' I had shouted, upon hearing the news. 'I will take such a husband as will make the King of France's head ache. Little he knows what a buffet I shall give him!'

The buffet was to be in the shape of the Earl of Arran, who was next in succession to the throne of Scotland. Cecil managed to get him smuggled out of France and into England as a suitor for my hand. I received Lord Arran in the garden at Hampton Court in a pretence of secrecy. It was diplomatic secrecy only, for I wished the tidings to run abroad as far as France and their French Majesties, thus to give them as much trouble and offence as they had given me. I heard that my cousin had burst into tears when she learned of it. No wonder, for if I married the Earl of Arran, I would have some title to the Scottish throne myself, through him. As it was, I found the gentleman not to my taste, being somewhat wild and overly dramatic in his manner. I refused his proposals, at which he seemed downcast, for indeed, 'twould have been a great thing for him. Instead, he made his way into Scotland, swearing to seize the Scottish throne and cause various troubles there, being eaten up with jealousy of Marie Stuart and beside himself with disappointment over his failure with me. I was very satisfied at this result of my policy, for it would serve to keep my cousin's eyes fixed on her own realm rather than on mine.

After the Earl of Arran came the Duke of Finland to sue for me on behalf of his brother, Eric, Crown Prince of Sweden. He was followed by the Duke of Holstein to speak yet again for the King of Denmark. So heated did these two become that they came near to blows in my presence, swearing, at dinner, to kill one another, knocking dishes to the floor, upsetting wine and bellowing like bulls in season.

'God's death!' I shrieked, jumping to my feet, scarce able to keep from laughing at the scuffling, the shouting, and the horrified faces turning this way and that to miss naught of such unseemly behaviour. 'What is this, before our face, sirs! Someone catch and hold these fierce gentlemen before they cut each other's throats under our eyes!'

There was Rob, red-faced and panting, endeavouring to restrain one, and two or three gents hanging on the arms of the other; such a kick-up, and all to get me for their masters. Oh, 'twas heady, 'twas thrilling, and I, until so lately in the shadow, loved it all. Almost drunken with it was I. Almost, but not quite. The fumes may have heated my blood, but never once did they cloud my brain. I needed all my powers for my statecraft, and although most others forgot this, never did I. Too much was at stake for that.

A merry time I had then, enjoying each day to the full. For, see'st thou, I had known no tender childhood, no joyous youth, only trouble and fears all my life until now. I meant to make up for all I had lacked and to lose no time in doing so. My suitors were not so merry, for they quarrelled and argued unceasingly while I delighted most naughtily to tease and flirt with them. Poor Cecil looked harassed almost to death at my behaviour, begging me to choose one and so leave the others honourably satisfied. But I would not and I could not, for I did not wish to wed, nor did I wish to range England on the side of anyone and thus against others, to her detriment. In my unmarried state I held a position of great power and was not minded to let it go. Greatly did I like to have all the threads of policy in my hands, weaving my way through plot and counter-plot, intrigue and secrecy, with faithful Cecil at my side. Less and less did I need him as guide, so quickly did I learn my part, but more and more as companion and colleague. Our minds matched fair and true, and this to his amaze, I being but a woman.

'Your Majesty has the mind of a man, and a great man, too,' he said to me one afternoon, as the days drew into winter. ' 'Tis extraordinary,' he went on, 'for I had thought the brains of women to be inferior to those of men. Indeed, for the most part, I do believe them to be so.'

'Well, my dear, if my brain be that of a

man, my body is assuredly that of a woman. I am a frivolous woman, moreover, loving finery, music, dance and flirtation.'

'You have had little enough such,' he answered warmly. ' 'Tis understandable.'

'Tonight we are to have a masked dance,' I told him, laughing excitedly. 'I am to go as Undine, the Water Princess, all in white and diamonds, with a green gauze robe over. And Cecil, I shall wear a green wig! What sayest thou to that? 'Tis curled all over, right down my back, and it becomes me mightily! Is it not a pretty fancy and a suitable trifle to amuse an inferior creature such as a woman?'

With a dancing step, I pranced out of the room, leaving him smiling and shaking his head as if he had ne'er met with such a being as I. Nor had he, I give you my word on that.

★ ★ ★

Rob and I talked much of our love in those bright months. He wished most ardently to marry me, and I — well, if I had a mind to take a husband 'twould have been he. Certes, my rank dazzled him, for he was an ambitious fellow and longed for power as had his dangerous father, the Duke of

Northumberland, before him. Yet he loved me greatly. I was his kind and drew him both physically and mentally. I was no helpless, clinging female; I was feared o' naught and growing more wilful and headstrong by the day. Now that there was no need to curb my temper, I let it have full sway and stamped and yelled as I wished. I took the reins from my tongue too, and spoke my mind straight. To remember myself so, it meseems that I was a very hell-cat, yet the number of those who truly loved me grew larger and larger. It was not all place-seeking, neither. One can tell. There is a spark in the eyes, a note in the voice, an odd sentence in the talk of those who love that is unmistakable to the loved one. Besides, I was a good judge of character; I had learned that in a hard school. Rob and I, we walked in the gardens at Placentia, we paced the Long Gallery at Richmond, we galloped in the park at Nonsuch, loitered by the river at Hampton, hunted at Windsor and Oatlands, sat by the fire at White Hall, and always we talked of this, our love.

'Nay, Rob, as to marriage! How can we marry? 'Tis stupid so to fret your mind with it. What of your wife? Have you forgot her, or do you mean to set up a seraglio like a Turk?'

'Oh, have done!' he snapped irritably. 'Am I ever likely to forget that I have a wife? The thought nags at me day and night. Would I *could* forget her! Would she never existed. Would she were — ' His words trailed off as he scowled into the fire, black brows drawn down, his mouth sullen.

'That is idle wish and dangerous,' said I. 'Let us speak of it no more.' I laid my hand on his. 'Darling Rob, can we not enjoy what we have and be thankful for it? God has given us much.'

'Ay, He has given *you* much indeed, and ice-water in your veins for blood, too. 'Tis easy for you to prate of thankfulness; you have reached the summit of your desires. I have not!' He seized my shoulders and my bones turned to milk as I looked into those hot, black eyes, alight with the flames of anger and desire. It was delicious to be grasped in his strong, young arms, to feel myself physically mastered. I sighed, gazing up at him, my eyes yearning, my mouth open, my whole body urgent for his love. We kissed and kissed, and thus entwined, would have retired to my chamber had not Kat come in, thinking the parlour empty. Rob cursed and flung out of the room, leaving me to smooth my ruffled hair and haul up my gown which had been dragged down nigh to my waist. I raised my brows at Kat's censorious expression.

'Well, Madam Virtue? What is your sermon for today?'

' 'Tis upon the dangers of playing with fire,' she said. 'Even Queens may be burned.'

I grinned at her. 'Is my hair tidy? Is my bodice straight? Even Queens are human.'

★ ★ ★

I shake my old head and smile now, when I think of those days long ago, when I was considered wild, immoral, uncontrollable and licentious by all the Courts of Europe. Not that these opinions held my suitors back, nay rather did it seem to increase their interest and wish to win me and my throne. My cousin, Marie Stuart, a wife, a Queen, though not yet a mother, was regarded as a model of all the feminine virtues, a pattern of propriety, sweet, biddable, gentle — all that a woman should be.

How she was to surprise and shock the world in years to come, when, compared with her scandals, mine were next to nothing! Poor fool, no one was more cruel to her than she was to herself, she having no idea of men and their motives and no understanding of human nature. She was sick most of her life, and I believe it affected her mind at times, unseating her already faulty judgment. Certes, she often acted as if her wits were gone. Some said the sickness was in her French royal blood, some said it was in her Tudor strain — for the Tudors were sickly and the Capets mad and sickly both. 'Tis not your true zany madness, this sickness, but accompanied by pain, swellings and fever, resulting in excitation of the brain. It is borne in the blood and passed on to a greater or lesser degree, and oft I ponder on the health of our families, now that I am in my old age.

I am alone now. Alone in spirit is what I mean, for there is none near me in intimacy except for my sweet cousin Kate Carey of Nottingham, daughter to my cousin Henry Carey. Life feels bleak and barren enough and sad enough too, although I have no desire at all to discover what waits for me hereafter. Old and weary and wheezing with the rheum as I am, I prefer to dwell in this sweet world. Dr. Dee has visited me again, good fellow that he is. So oft have I promised him preferment and somehow always have put it off until later. I must bestir myself to find him a place, for he deserves it, God knows. He has ever bestirred himself for me. Mayhap I will do so when the weather is warmer and I feel more like myself.

What would you say, my Rob, could you see me now? Would you fall back in dismay at my wrinkled cheeks and sunken, toothless mouth, or would you greet me with love and swear that I looked not a day older than when you last beheld me? Oh yes, you would greet me with the blind eyes of love, as well I know, my dear, my dearest. Would you were with me still . . .

★ ★ ★

I gave Rob some goodly gifts in that first year of my reign. Well, and why not? I could do more for him in that way than he could do for me. I gave him the Garter, and to go with it, a mansion at Kew, lands, a paid office, and a licence to export woollen cloth free of all duty. The last was a gift of love. By this, he would have ready money constantly at hand and rich profits in the future. As well as these, he received 1,000 marks a year from his Mastership of the Horse, so he was well able to hold his head up amongst his fellows and put on as brave a show as any.

He saw but little of Amye, his wife, although he visited her at Denchworth occasionally. Once she came to London to see him, but for the most part she wandered about the country, visiting and staying with friends. Rob said she fretted for him, but of a truth, her lot was no different from that of any lady whose husband had a place at Court. Courtiers' wives were asked there only if they were to be the Sovereign's personal attendants, and in this case, nothing could have been less likely! Rob did not set her up in a large establishment, where she could live in state and comfort and where he could stay when on leave from Court, because she did not wish the responsibility of such a home, saying that she knew not how to manage so many servants or carry out the requisite duties. She preferred to stay with her friends at Denchworth. She had no spirit, said Rob in irritation, no force of character, being meek, retiring, wincing and clinging enough to drive him crazy. She made him feel right guilty, he said, and that filled him with anger against himself and her, for what had seemed so shy and appealing at seventeen, seemed not at all so at twenty-six, after nine years of marriage.

'We do not suit,' he said, exasperated, 'and have not ever done, in truth, poor soul. I was young and driven by lust only, mistaking it for love. 'Tis no different from many marriages where husband and wife are better apart. Yet, by the Lord, it was a mighty mistake. No one forced me to it, it was not arranged; I did it all of my own will and have no one to blame but myself, curse it. That makes it all the worse. I wish I had never laid eyes on the poor wretch, indeed I do. I wish she had never been born. Oh Bess, she keeps me from you!'

'How so?' I teased. 'You are here with me, are you not? Here, in my chamber, upon my bed, with the curtains drawn and good Tamworth outside the door for safety. You should pay that man a high wage, Rob. His silence is worth a Kingdom.'

'Never mind Tamworth. Hearken to what I say. Amye keeps me from you, and you know full well what I mean. I would marry you, my adored one, my beautiful, my own woman. I long for it more than life.'

'Well, 'tis impossible, so speak of it no more. It cannot be, Rob. I am the Queen of England and you have a wife already. Let us enjoy what we have and forget this doleful dump. If you do not, I will leave you here and call for Kat to dress me. Then I will have music and I will dance with any gent who takes my fancy. There are other men at Court, thou knowest, though none as handsome, I grant, who are merry and not gloomy — ' I gave a delighted shriek as he snatched me, covering my face with kisses and throwing me back on the bed.

'Witch! Bitch!' he growled in my ear. 'Trifle with me, would you? Tease and play with me, ha? Take this and this and this!' These were kisses resulting in bruises upon my neck and bosom which took some skill in covering later, sweet marks that they were.

To divert the interest of others from our love affair, Rob joined his sister Mary in approving the idea of my marriage to the Archduke Charles of Austria, Bishop De Quadra was delighted for a space, thinking me as good as won, while Rob's jealous enemies at Court were hoodwinked into silence for a time. Even dear, worried Cecil forgot to cluck and shake his head at my fondness for The Gipsy, as Rob was called. 'Twas greatly amusing, but not long to last, for in November, De Quadra fairly cornered me for a definite answer.

'Well, Bishop,' I said, chuckling, 'Lord Robert cannot read my mind, nor can Lady Mary, his sister. Indeed, I do not know my own on this subject yet. It needs much careful thought and consideration, for 'tis a mighty matter with far-reaching consequences.' And I refused to say more, persuade me though he tried.

Many Catholic nobles who had been pleased at the thought of my marriage with the Archduke were enraged with Rob for deceiving them and thus raising their hopes of a Catholic alliance. The Duke of Norfolk and Rob had a noisy quarrel about it; swords were whipped out, and in a flash, both were ready to fight until dragged apart with cries off: 'Put up! Put up!' and the like.

' 'Tis plain!' yelled the Duke, as he was pulled away. ' 'Tis plain that if the Queen marry not outside England, she must marry inside, and that if she marry inside, her choice would fall on you. So, by tricks, you try to keep the way clear! What of your wife, I say? What of your wife?'

There was uproar, and many small fist fights broke out. I had much ado to quieten the storm, threatening imprisonment, chains, the Tower, at the top of my voice. It was all very difficult. I would not wed the Archduke though I could, but I needed his friendship and that of Spain. I could not wed Rob if I would, for he had a wife, and for an hundred other reasons, the chiefest being that I was mortal afeared of marriage and all it entailed.

So the uneasy situation continued. As the months went by, I knew that it must resolve itself somehow. I could not dismiss Rob; I adored him, so comely, his princely grace, his effortless beauty was happiness to me.

He was a true man in every way, dear, dear Rob. The gossip grew stronger; 'twas repeated that we were secretly wed, that I was pregnant, that I had borne a child by him. It began to prey upon my nerves and my temper grew short. I suffered vilely from headaches and had many a fit of weeping. I snapped and snarled at everyone, even Rob himself. I wanted him so much. My heart longed to submit, my woman's blood urged me to make myself his own. Yet my mind and my Queenship would brook no mastery of me. And Rob himself was not one to sit at home all day amongst the cinders. He was proud and possessive; he would seek to rule me. He sought to rule me even now. Why, he tried to give his orders to my servants before all. I flew into a towering rage at this, one day, hurling my new feather fan to the floor and stamping until my foot hurt.

'God's death!' I screamed, shrill as any peacock. 'Do you think to take place of me, my Lord? I tell you, my favour is not so locked up for you that others shall not partake thereof! If you think to rule here, I will take a course to see you forthcoming! I will have here but one mistress and no master! Do you hear? Do you hear?' I yelled after him, for, amidst horrified gasps, he had flung round and marched straight out

112

of the hall, turning his back upon me, his Sovereign, and kicking the door shut with a crash.

His Sovereign leaped down the steps of her dais and rushed after him. 'Come back!' I bawled. 'Come here, I say! Lord Robert, on pain of banishment, I bid you stand!' He stood, scowling, and glared at me. I dealt him a hearty blow on the cheek. 'Take that!' I shouted. 'Remember, I am your Queen!'

He caught my wrists in his hands. 'And you would do well to remember it also, Madam,' he ground out between shut teeth, ' 'stead of ranting and railing like a fishwife!'

'I will send you to the Tower! I will have you in irons — '

'Ay, you can do as you will; you have the power. I am naught against you, as well I know. I am but a man who loves you!' he roared furiously. 'Your mammet to be jeered at by your courtiers! Oh, never look so amazed. 'Tis so, is it not?'

'I have raised you up; I can cast you down!'

'Why do you not, then?'

For answer, I burst into tears and could not stop. My ladies came running up, dismayed, but my head was on Rob's shoulder and I heeded them not. His arm was about me, his hand stroking my hair.

'Shall I send them away, my Queen?' he said gently.

'Ay, do so,' I sobbed. 'Oh, Rob, my head whirls. What ails me?'

'You need what all women need, my dear one; love, a husband, children. Their lack works upon your spirit.' He handed me his kerchief and I mopped my eyes.

'Ay, but I cannot, I cannot, Rob! I cannot endure a master, and I am mortal feared of wedding. It means more to me than you know. At my age, most women are years wed, with half-grown sons and large families. All this has passed me by. I have had no real youth, no gaiety, no place, even, until now, and this place I have I would not lose. If I marry, he whom I wed would seek to rule me, he would seek to be King. He would come between me and my realm. You know it is so.'

He nodded. 'You are overwrought,' he said soothingly. 'Come, let us go to your chamber, sweeting. What say you?'

He did not understand, that was plain. No one understood that I, a woman, truly wished to remain unwed. I gave a sharp sigh and sank down upon a settle, Rob with me, my hand in his. 'Nay, Rob,' I replied, ' 'tis not in my heart just now. See'st thou, love, there is much pressure upon me to marry. It drives me near crazy. Do you not comprehend that I have a true horror of the state?' I shook my head at his face of disbelief. 'Moreover, whoever I wed will seek dominion over me in England. That I will not have. Besides which, if I did marry, and I think I shall not, I want no foreign husband or a stranger. Do you not *see*, Rob?' I cried in exasperation. 'I want — '

'I know what you want,' he whispered. 'Come, darling, let us — '

It was useless. I jumped to my feet. 'Nay, Rob, I would ride. Order up the horses for you, for me, and a small company. Look not so cast down, sweetheart, we can outride them all an we wish.'

And with that, my darling had to be content.

Sure, Rob loved my Queenship and his hopes of glory thereby. It was natural enough. I bore him no ill-feeling for that; I understood it. But he loved me as a woman too. I was his kind. He had a predilection for women like me; my bright colouring, my vitality, my lithe athletic slimness and grace of movement so like his own, my physical courage, my sudden wild rages and equally wild response to his love. My force of character appealed to him even while it enraged him, my love of sport and movement, my sense of drama and display all matched his. Even the shadow upon my birth attracted him, for there was also a cast upon his own ancestry, and we had each lost a parent, by the axe. Oh ay, we were like and like. Added to this, I was the daughter of a King, and a Queen in my own right. It was a heady mixture and wrought hotly upon the handsome, black-browed, dashing Lord Robert Dudley, may his gallant soul rest in Paradise.

'They say he is thinking of divorcing his wife,' said Katey, one March evening as I made ready for bed.

'They say!' I repeated scornfully. 'Who are these 'they' who are such busy talkers? If he thinks in such wise, he will have to think again.'

'Well, but your Majesty's royal father — '

'And that is why he must think again, stupid! After my father's matrimonial adventures, the Church and my people will stand for no more. Their wishes must be respected. Have those people not put me where I am today? No more on the subject, Katey. I am sick of it.'

So the matter rested, for there were other things to occupy me. My army had gone into Scotland to assist the Protestant Scots to rid themselves of the French. Philip of Spain was troubled at this, for, although he hated the French, he hated Protestants more. He began to threaten us, and to avert possible disaster from this direction, I had to make public avowal to wed the Archduke Charles, which was annoying, although I had no doubt of my ability to deal with that when the time came. It was bothersome, none the less, for I hated to make too many definite statements in policy.

I was worried too, about that army in Scotland, for there had been a defeat at Leith, and expensive reinforcements had to be sent which the Treasury could ill afford. The whole affair cost us £688,000, a whole year's revenue, and it seemed to me a monstrous wastage. I was furious when I heard the total. But better fortune came to follow this reverse, for Mary of Guise, the French mother of the Queen of Scots and Queen-Regent of Scotland, lay a-dying, causing the French to think more of their own affairs than ours. Callous I may seem, to have regarded this death as good fortune, but I could not stay her dying and was right glad for French eyes to be turned elsewhere for a while.

It was the struggles of the great City financier Tom Gresham, Cecil and me, to put the national monetary system on a workable basis after such a drain of resources, that earned me the first of my reputation for parsimony in governmental matters. I was forced to it in these my early days as Queen, yet some of my cautious grandsire Henry VII must have been in me, for I found it not difficult to save. The habit did grow on me, I confess, but I have never been a lavish spender, not even upon myself, preferring to hoard and save and amass money thereby. Wealth is power, no two ways about it.

I liked Gresham. His strong rugged face and bright blue eyes appealed to me. His agile brain and acute business sense I found even more fascinating. I recall that this was the year that he suffered severe injuries through a fall from his horse. He was lame ever after, poor Tom, but thanks be to God, his wits were unimpaired. A true friend he ever stood to England and me.

3

GREATEST SCANDAL WAITS ON GREATEST STATE

1560 – 1561

In June, sweet month of roses, came the news that my forces had taken Edinburgh, and a month later a treaty was concluded there which banished all threat of a French invasion by way of Scotland and brought us peace in the north. Under the terms of this treaty, the King and Queen of France were to give up the English Royal Arms, my title as Queen was to be properly recognised, and the French soldiers were to be withdrawn from Scotland. This document was to be ratified by Marie herself. My Cecil was principal in drawing up this treaty, and rode down in triumphant haste from Edinburgh to me at Hampton Court to apprise me of it in detail.

Poor man, he met with an unkind reception, I fear me, monster of ingratitude that I was, for I was near demented with nervous fret after a ferocious quarrel with

119

Rob, who had threatened to leave Court against my express wish, and even now was flouting me by remaining shut in his room. He had uttered wild and foolish words against his wife, against the Archduke, even against me. He shouted that I treated him as a toy and no man, that he refused to be my lap-dog. He would kidnap me, force me to his will, make me pregnant, and so constrain me to marry him. After this, there would be little outcry against his divorce from Amye, such was his rash reasoning.

I felt beleaguered and desperate, in a whirl of conflicting emotions, and instead of praising Cecil's brilliance and diplomacy, railed and wept like a spoiled child, ordering him from me without thought or consideration. He went, but not before I had heard him mutter under his breath that he wished Lord Robert Dudley in Paradise. I snatched off a shoe and hurled it at his retreating back, but it struck the door as he closed it softly behind him. Then I wept more bitterly than ever. He put me first, did my Spirit, afore his own wife and family. He needed my preferment for their sakes, and I needed his presence for mine own. Also, I loved him dearly, so my tears were for very shame and regret. But he always made allowance for me, most devoted of men that he was, and we reconciled our difference speedily, I saw to that.

At the end of this fretful and vexing month of August, I moved myself and my Court to Windsor, but I found no peace there, neither. Cecil protested to me about my continual favouring of Lord Robert, offering to leave my side and retire from our work if I conducted myself to his Lordship in such fashion. I was enraged, and shouted that I would do as I pleased and would brook no interference from those who wished to rule me, and in two minutes Cecil and I were at outs again. I felt ready to split in two. I could not give Robert up, he meant too much to me, yet I had no intention of allowing him to spoil my destiny. Something would have to happen, I felt. It was as if a storm were brewing and ready to erupt upon us.

On the 8th of September, the day after my twenty-seventh birthday, Amye Dudley was dead. The news burst like a thunderclap over the Court and then over the whole country. Sweet Jesu, what a scandal it was! My head reels still when I recall it. The shock was so great that I was as one stunned or drunken, and knew not what to think or say. Wild ideas and furious fancies rushed through my mind. Was she murdered, or did she die by her own hand? Was Rob behind it? Had he planned it? Had he hired bravos to do it? Christ, how could I wed him now? How could I show him any feeling or favour hereafter? Oh God and all angels, would any think that I, the Queen, had been a party to it?

I swayed back, catching the curtains to save me from falling, while the vista of trees and grass in the park advanced and receded alarmingly. Kat helped me to a chair, where I sat collapsed, my hands over my face. She called for hot wine and tried to soothe me. I would have none of my ladies nigh me, only my Kat, she who had shared all my fortunes and fears. I rocked myself back and forth, my faculties all suspended, my heart beating heavily, my breath coming short and quick. I did not swoon, that was not my way, but surely came close to it. The hot spiced wine revived me, but I trembled as if I had a fever and stared at Kat like one in a trance.

'God's death!' I whispered at last. 'What's to do, Kat? What in Heaven's name's to do?'

She swallowed and said hesitatingly: 'Sweeting, were you privy to it?' Dumbly, I shook my head. ''Twill be said you were.'

'I knew nothing of it,' I gasped. 'Nothing. Was it a plot? Was it an accident? How did she die?'

'She was found dead at the bottom of the stairs, with her neck broke.'

'Jesu! Where was she lodging? Where were her people, that this should happen?'

'Why, she was lodging at Cumnor Hall, near Abingdon in Oxfordshire.'

'Not with the Hydes, then?'

'Oh nay, she had left Denchworth. And 'tis said she was all alone in the house.'

'Alone? How so?'

'She had sent all her people to the fair.'

'All?'

'Everyone.'

I shook my head. I could not understand any of it. 'Who found her?'

'Lord Robert's kinsman, Thomas Blount, met a servant called Bowes who had found her and was riding hard to tell Lord Robert the news.'

'Good God, it is past belief! Kat, I must see Lord Robert at once. Fetch him now, here to me. I must think of something. He cannot stay at Windsor, that is sure.'

Kat returned swiftly with Rob, having met him on the way. He looked distracted and fell on his knees beside my chair. 'Elizabeth! You have heard?'

I signed to Kat to leave us. 'Now, Rob, you must tell me all you know. All, I say, be it never so bad.'

'Amye is dead, you know that?' I nodded, and he hurried on, 'I know not how, I swear it. Bowes said her neck was broke and she alone in the house. 'Tis thought that Forster — '

'Forster?'

'Ay, Forster, my treasurer, who took Cumnor Hall on my behalf, some years agone. 'Tis whispered he knows somewhat.'

'Where is it whispered?'

'In Abingdon. Tom Blount found out that much.'

'What has this Forster to say to anything?'

'I know not. He and his wife live at Cumnor with a sister of the Hydes called Mrs. Odingsells. But they were all at the fair except Amye. 'Twill be said that I instructed Forster to kill her.'

'Did you, Rob?'

'Never upon my life!'

I wrung my hands together. 'You must leave Windsor today,' I said.

'Leave Windsor? I am guiltless! I swear to you — '

'Never mind swearing, Rob. You must go. Great heavens, should you stay here, it will be rumoured that you and I plotted this between us! Rob, I am the Queen. I must not seem to condone aught, even suspicion, in our case. There has been enough talk

124

about us as it is. Go to Kew. It must be seen that I have sent you, and you must be under house-arrest. Stay there quiet, I charge you.'

So to Kew perforce he went, and I out a-hunting to clear my troubled mind. Rob had told me that he had sent off a letter to Tom Blount at Abingdon, bidding him charge the Coroner to choose honest and upright men to serve on the jury at the enquiry into the cause of Amye's death. He had also sent another courier to her family in Norfolk, summoning them to be present at the inquest, so that they be privy to all procedures. He was no fool, realising that openness was the best course in so dreadful an affair.

Bishop De Quadra had arrived at Windsor two days before the tragedy, and was like a ferret over it, eyes a-gleam, long nose a-twitch to scent out scandals. When I spoke to him, his excitement was ill-concealed under a spurious gravity of demeanour. What a luscious snippet for King Philip, his master! What a wondrous chance to discredit me in the eyes of Spain and the world, to drive a wedge between me and the love of my people and thus leave the way open to a Spanish invasion, perchance! Surrounded by his Spaniards, he asked me if I knew the manner of Lady Dudley's death. I answered that she has broken her neck. '*Si ha rotto il collo*,' I said in Italian for immediate privacy, continuing in the same tongue to ask him not to noise it abroad too loud. It would be loud enough presently, I said.

Well, such a thing could not be kept secret. Everyone was talking of it, from Scotland to France. All manner of rumours were bandied about, and pretty rumours they were! It was said that I had a child by Robert, that he had killed his own wife to take a royal one, that he and I would end in the Tower, and on and on, more and more scurrilous. I knew well that, in people's minds, all Queens must not only be beautiful, but virtuous also. 'Tis necessary in a goddess-symbol, such as I was beginning to be seen. Unclean goddesses are in a fair way to be cast out. Folk do not like their heroines smirched. Frantic I felt, but it would never do to show it, so I did my best to preserve a cool demeanour, realising that the less I knew of the whole business the better. My Ambassadors were in a ferment. Thomas Randolph wrote in a frenzy from Edinburgh, thinking my marriage to Robert imminent now that Amye was dead. Randolph begged the Council to use any means to stop this fateful wedding. Throckmorton wrote from Paris, imploring

Cecil to hinder any wedding, and wished that he might crawl away somewhere and die for very shame. The expectation of my marriage had ruined all the triumph of our Scottish victories, he wrote, adding that the King and Queen of France were refusing to ratify the Treaty of Edinburgh, believing that internal dissatisfaction and loss of face abroad would render England unable to enforce the Treaty. England was laughed at, he wrote, her Queen reviled and threatened, her religion mocked.

I heard that my dear cousin Marie was much amused by my trouble, having laughed aloud when told of it. 'The Queen of England is going to marry her Horse-Keeper who has killed his wife to make room for her!' she cried gaily. It did not endear her to me, being both tasteless and insulting, I felt, and showing a remarkable lack of restraint and diplomacy. Yet I had to bear it, bitter though it was. Cecil spared me none of it, nor should he have done so. It was right that I should know, for not only was I head of the State, but of the Church too, guardian of men's immortal souls and basis of their earthly future. I understood this but too well and felt my throne shake beneath me, though I showed not my fear. I held fast to my belief in Rob's innocence, both in public and in private. Here, Cecil was of great help to me, for he seemed to share my belief, even visiting Rob at Kew, kindly and upon my behalf. He had known as I had, that Amye had been ailing for some time from a pain in her breast, and seemed willing to give Rob the benefit of the doubt. Rob wrote him a most grateful letter, asking his advice upon what he should do.

I put the Court into mourning for Lady Dudley, and asked one of my oldest friends to represent me at her funeral. For this unwanted task I chose the daughter of Lord Williams of Thame who had befriended me in my young days of travail. She had been a good comrade to me this many a year and was wed to Sir Henry Norris, the son of him who had been beheaded under suspicion of having been my mother's lover so many years before. I had a marked kindness for him as well as all the Williams family. They still lived at Rycote in Oxfordshire, and were most loyal, loving and true. Through my fondness for nicknames, Lady Norris was known to me and all her family as Black Crow, for indeed, she was as dark as any crow with her black hair and eyes and olive skin. Rycote was near to where the ceremony was to be held, so my Crow would not be put to too much trouble on my behalf.

Nevertheless, in spite of my care to uphold

the conventions, it was confidently predicted that I was in a fair way to lie down The Queen, and wake next morning but Madame Elizabeth, I and my paramour with me. Was there ever such a coil? I knew not what to do about any of it. If I married Robert, it would seem that I believed not in his innocence. I was not sure that I wished to wed him in any event; I knew not my own mind at this time, for longing and expedience fought an equal battle. Not all the great folk in England were against him neither, for some felt that if I wedded the man I loved it would be the best way to get a prince for England, and would thus serve and honour Rob. The matter roiled on, this way and that. I held fast to it that I believed absolutely in Rob's innocence and seized every opportunity to say so, but I wished not to know too much, in case — in case . . .

I slept but little and ate less, for I was much saddened and perplexed. At times I felt that I had been within an ace of marrying Rob, at others I recoiled from the idea. I swore to myself that I had never swerved from my original intention of remaining unwed, only to be at once overcome by an agonising wave of desire. I could never marry him now, I protested. *Why not?* I thought, moments later. Nay, marriage was a trap and this was a warning. I had best send him away and cease to torture myself and him, I reflected agitatedly.

But I allowed him to return to Court, toying with the notion of reinstating him publicly. I decided to give him the earldom that he craved, but when the warrant was brought to me, that November of 1560, I read it through, fidgeted with it, picked up my pen, chewed the feather all irresolute, finally laying the pen down. *Stay Bess, thought I, you do this and all will believe 'twas a plot 'twixt you and him to kill Amye, else why should he be so favoured?*

'Nay,' I said aloud. 'Nay!' and seizing my coral-handled penknife, cut the parchment to pieces.

In the latter part of the same month, news came from France that the young King Francis lay sick of the earache. In him, it was no light matter, for he was an unhealthy creature, some saying he had leprosy, but this was never proven. Bedford's daughter, Ann Russell, whispered, round-eyed, that he needed to bathe in the blood of babies for a cure.

'Oh, horrible!' shuddered Kat. 'What a monster he must be. And so young!'

I laughed loudly at this. 'Kat, do not heed such parlous rubbish! Poor lad, he hath a poisoned ear which is mightily swelled and purulent. 'Tis said he is in great pain.'

'Will he die, think you, Madam?' asked Ann, curiously.

'Who can tell? One thing I do know is that if he does die, there will be no room for my smug little cousin in France. She will be sent swift on her way to her cold and mountainous Kingdom of Scotland, there to be a sore nuisance to me, I'll warrant!'

God's teeth, how right I was! I must have been struck by the gift of prophecy, for that cousin of mine grew to be a very thorn in my side and remained so for the rest of her turbulent, ill-omened life. Through her I may be misjudged through history, through her the peace of my realm was threatened and my policy of religious tolerance well-nigh set at naught. She brought happiness to no one, least of all to herself.

Here at home, gossip still ran rife. Rob was back at Court, following the Coroner's verdict of accidental death, but I bade him act as meek as possible, for he had enemies enough, through jealousy of my favour, without the making of more. He liked it not, and ever was I glimpsing his sullen visage glowering through the throng, for I would not call him too soon to my side. Mighty bad did this restraint work upon our tempers which were never of the sweetest at their best. I longed for him and my ladies suffered a deal with my tantrums as a result. I heard them whisper that I was as fierce as my father, even to his habit of striking out and throwing objects when in a rage. This, I confess, gave me a sneaking pleasure, to feel that I was like him. Well, I had spent too many years denying my true self, not to allow it free expression now. I said and did exactly as I pleased. I also wore what I pleased, discovering in myself a love of finery as glittering as my great father ever had. There were many wondrous jewels, left by him, my brother and my sister, for me to wear, and I hung myself about with them until I shone like a galaxy. I wore rings upon all my long and lovely fingers, even upon my thumbs. There were some vinegar-faces who raised their brows at me and my doings, but what of that? Supreme power in the land was I, and soon all the world would know it. Now was my turn to call the tune and all would dance to it as long as I should live. I would ride out this unlucky turn, although my dear people might mutter and look askance over this wretched Amye Dudley; I would show them that scandal might brush me but lightly, then pass on for ever. And so it happened in the end.

Nigh unto Christmas came more news of the French King. He had died on the fifth of December, in torment from his rotten ear. Humours had swelled up behind it and could not be released. Instead, his wife was released, to my douleur, and eventually, her own. Again, the marriage-mongers were busy about me, saying that I had best wed to secure the Succession as a protection against the Queen of Scots. My Councillors said it to my face, my ladies whispered it, twitter-twittering of it at one end of the chamber as if I were deaf, as I wrote my letters, sitting by the fire, my father's desk open upon a convenient small table.

'God's death!' I cried, throwing down my pen, so that they all jumped, startled. 'Will you never have done? No heir, indeed! What of Lady Catherine Grey? So, no answer! Are you all struck dumb as well as stupid?'

'Lady Catherine?' stammered Ann Russell. 'Lady Jane Grey's sister?'

'Lady Catherine, certainly,' I said. 'She is next heir under my father's will. Hast forgotten that? She is a fool, I grant, being both self-important and easily-led, but my heir for all that.'

'But we thought you so fond of her,

dearest,' protested Katey Knollys. 'You pay her so much attention.'

'Ach, 'tis to keep her quiet and mollified. De Feria had ideas of a marriage between her and the Archduke Charles, or even Spanish Philip's son, a while ago. Now do you understand? She could plunge us into a peck of trouble. I do not wish her to grow too friendly with De Quadra and mayhap complain to him that she gets short shrift from me. This might revive ideas of a Spanish marriage for her. 'Tis a devilish nuisance, and so is she.'

'But poor little Lady Jane, her sister,' said Kat sorrowfully. 'That was a sad case, was it not?'

'Indeed so, poor child, and it was her foolish father's fault entirely. God knows what my fat cousin, her mother, is plotting at this moment, untrustworthy bitch that she is!'

'Her Grace of Suffolk, mean you?'

'Ay, Mistress Stokes herself,' I answered on a crack of laughter.

'Yea,' giggled Ann. 'She wed her grooms-man but three weeks after her husband was executed. A man half her age, is he not?'

'Red-haired and lusty,' nodded Katey, 'with an eye to the main chance and an ear for the rattle of well-filled money-bags.'

'She lies ill now,' put in Kat. ' 'Tis thought she may not recover.'

'God grant her a place in Heaven,' said I, 'although I doubt it.'

★ ★ ★

I stared drowsily into the fire, remembering. Exciting days were those, and I as resilient as a steel spring. I had need to be i' faith for I filled a man's place and none knew me as they do now. Handsome I was too, ay, or near it enough to pass for such. My teeth were still good then, without gaps or blackening. Without the toothache, too. God's mercy, I suffer it now; hearty pangs in my old gums. But the toothdrawing is worse than the toothache to my mind. I have felt both and I know. Ay indeed. Of what was I thinking but a moment agone? Hey, but my memory is not what it was. 'Tis terrible to grow old. Ah, now I have it, 'twas of the Amye Dudley business and those times after. Well, I recovered from it all as time passed. One does as time passes. The Christmas of that year came and went, and Twelfth Night, and I dared to hope that the sorry scandals were beginning to grow less.

I could bear no discussion on the subject and forbade any to speak of it on pain of my severe displeasure. So matters went on and the months rolled by. The business of Marie Stuart's widowhood I found useful, in one way, for it served to draw off the interest and speculation from the Amye Dudley affair, and focus it on another, which was a great relief to me.

Money was very scant after the Scottish war of the previous year, while a disastrous dearth in the same summer had made bread vilely scarce and expensive for poor folk. It was God's blessing that I had inherited my grandsire's financial ability. I had come to a poverty stricken Kingdom whose wealth had been wasted through three reigns, and near all my personal monies went to bolster up the empty coffers of my country and to help the starving and needy. I knew that a poor realm was a weak one, and so every penny must be put to good use. Some state gowns I had to have, and some fine furniture, in order to make a good impression upon the foreign ambassadors, for it would never do for them to be writing despatches to their masters that England's Queen was hard put to it in any matter, least of all money. I wished to create an illusion of power. This, in time, was to become no illusion but truth, but those days were not yet. New Year was always the best time, for while I gave the clergy and nobles gilt plate from my store according to their rank, they gave me money on the same scale. This did assist my desperate finances most greatly, and none seemed to grudge the giving, or did not show it. All gave and received gifts on New Year's Day.

One gift I had that year was not of money. It was a pair of black silk knit stockings I had from Mrs. Montague, the first I had ever seen. When I put them on, they fitted my legs like another skin and drove Rob nigh crazy. Until then, I had possessed many pairs of pretty stockings in coloured and embroidered taffety, but being cut in two pieces and seamed up the fronts and backs of the legs, they wrinkled sadly. But there, that had ever been the fault of hosen, garter them tight as one could. Now, in these black charmers, my legs would be as elegant as they were made to be, and full high did I hold my skirts in the dance, or when mounting steps and the like.

I wore a green pair at the water party Rob gave on the Thames on Midsummer Day. Most fetching they looked and I made much play with my green and white satin skirts, lifting them naughtily high from my green shod feet to show my neat silken ankles. We were all in boats, eating, drinking, singing, even dancing though stately-wise. Small craft filled with singers and musicians followed us, taking care not to strike the wine bottles hanging upon cords in the water to keep cool. It was a pretty scene, for the boats were all of different colours, silvered and gilded and garlanded with fresh flowers. My boat was of purple and gold and the flowers upon it were roses and forget-me-nots. Rob and I were leaning upon the rail, whispering and laughing, when De Quadra passed by us and bowed. Rob raised his goblet and called merrily to De Quadra to drink to the beauty of my legs in their silken hosen. I lifted my skirt provocatively to show my feet and legs above the ankle to the Spaniard, whose eyes gleamed appreciatively.

'Ah, *si* — very beautiful,' he said. '*Muy bella!*'

'Oh, my Lord,' I gurgled, 'and you a bishop! You should have cast your eyes down *modestamente* and affected not to notice *cosas tanpiarescas como piernas* — such wanton things as legs!'

'Nay, why should he not? They are enough to drive a man to desperation!' cried Rob boldly, kissing my cheek and laying his arm about my waist. I leaned my head against his shoulder, glancing saucily up at him.

'Stay Rob, what will the good Bishop think of such forwardness?' I laughed. 'He will deem me no virgin an I allow you to take such liberties in action and speech with me.'

'Hey, but he can remedy that, sweeting,' riposted Robert. 'The Bishop might as well marry us here and now, for he is fitted for such office. What say you, my Lord? Will you wed us?'

'Impossible!' I cried giggling. 'Bishop De Quadra cannot speak enough English to perform the wedding service, and you, Rob, cannot speak Spanish. I would have to act as interpreter for both. Indeed, I would have no time, in all the translating, to make mine own responses. Mayhap the Lord Bishop and Rob would find themselves wed to one another in error!' Although Rob and I laughed heartily, De Quadra said quite seriously in his halting English that he would be glad to marry us, but for one thing. 'And what is that?' I asked, jestingly.

'*Cuando Vuestra Majestad haya apartado a Cecil y su grupo de herejes de suspuestos alrededor de Vuestra Majestad y Lord Roberto donde cuando deseen,*' he said rapidly to me, wholly in earnest, his glowing dark eyes fixed meaningly upon mine.

'Come, what says he?' cried Rob eagerly.

'Why, he offers to marry me to Lord Robert!' I called gaily. There was at once a gasp of dismay, a hubbub of protest, and a single delighted shout from Rob. 'But that is not all,' I went on, mischievously. 'To achieve this, I must rid myself of Cecil and his gang of heretics who surround my person.'

There were cries of 'Oh!' and 'Shame!' and general laughter. I shook my head, smiling at De Quadra, who shrugged resignedly. 'Nay, I cannot do that,' said I. 'Cecil knows all my secrets, and that gang of heretics as you call them, why they serve me as well as they do, Bishop, because they would rather have me than any other. 'Tis the power of my legs in silk stockings, see'st thou. No heretic is proof against them!'

During the merriment that followed this, I glanced at Rob standing crestfallen by the boat-rail where I had left him, and extended my hand. He came to me and took it. I did not wish to make him look foolish or to wound him, for he loved me sore and had spent much on this water-party to devise it to my liking. 'I shall not give up;' he grumbled, as we walked slowly astern. 'I mean to win you if I can.'

'Well, 'tis in God's hands,' I replied, sighing piously. 'He is better fit to deal with such a matter than I.'

4

OH, CONTENTIOUS, CAPTIOUS COUSINS!

1561 – 1562

If I had believed in signs and portents, I would have been greatly overset by an event which had occurred on the fourth of June 1561. There was a great and terrible storm in which the hand of God was clearly seen by those inclined that way. The church of St. Martin Ludgate was struck by a lightning bolt, the flames of the conflagration leaping up the hill like the wings of some avenging angel to envelop the ancient wooden steeple of St. Paul's. The fire raged for four hours, despite the rain; the bells melted, the lead poured in torrents from the roof which finally fell in, reducing the proudest cathedral in England to a partial ruin. Distinct earth tremors were felt, and loud were the cries of 'witch-craft!' and 'sorcery!' The Protestants blamed the Catholics for God's displeasure thus clearly shown, while the Catholics were no less vociferous upon the subject of God's dislike of the Protestants. Both factions united in declaring it 'a judgment'.

Judgment or no, it was a disaster and likely to cause expense, which I saw as a greater disaster. Natheless, I gave a great deal of money and timber to aid repairs. I could ill afford it, but it was necessary, for St. Paul's was the heart of London; the very crucible of worship. It was the responsibility of the Sovereign as well as of the City. The aldermen and City fathers gave a large sum, and the clergy too. All this wrought together so well that in but one month a false roof was up and work progressing fast.

As well as expenses, I had much to worry and upset me that summer. The great cause of it lay with Lady Jane Seymour, a Maid of Honour of mine, since dead, and my cousin Catherine Grey. I had been very fond of Lady Jane, a daughter of my brother's uncle, the one-time Lord Protector of England, favouring her much, and had no idea that she had been aiding her brother, the young Lord Hertford, to court Catherine Grey. Catherine's mother, my first cousin, the fat and bad-tempered Duchess of Suffolk, had, as I later discovered, instigated the whole affair. It was kept all secret from me, and with good reason, for I would have stopped it, or at least wished to have somewhat to say in the marriage of my heir.

As it turned out, Frances of Suffolk died very soon after her promotion of this match, and Lady Catherine and her sister Lady Mary were left, motherless, fatherless and wellnigh dowerless, a charge on me which I fully accepted, expensive though it was to keep the two girls in their proper condition. Besides, I felt sorry for the two unfortunate girls, even though they irritated me. They were blood relatives, after all.

The secret affair crept on. Lady Jane Seymour managed most of it, even to bringing in a clergyman to wed the couple, she herself acting as the only witness. The wedding had taken place in Lord Hertford's lodging during the winter and none knew of it. Even the bride and groom did not know the name of the cleric who married them, he being afeared of my displeasure should I discover the match. In March, Lady Jane, delicate like all the Seymour women, suddenly died. Being much attached to her, I gave her a great state funeral in Westminster Abbey. No evil attended her death, it was a natural one, for she had ailed all her life. I missed her, for she had been a link of sorts between me and my little brother.

A short time after this, I appointed Lord Hertford on a mission to France, and off he went, leaving his wife alone, and me none the wiser as to his wedded state. I had no notion of Catherine's case, except that she seemed ever doleful and inclined to tears. This I put down to grief over the death of her close friend. Needless to say, she was pregnant and at desperate pains to conceal it.

During July and August I went on Progress into Essex and Suffolk feeling irritable and depressed, for my Councillors never let the marriage question rest and it caused me much misery and unease. Even dear old Dr. Matthew Parker, whom I had made Archbishop of Canterbury, and who accompanied me on this Progress at my express wish, could not leave the subject alone. When I wept, and confessed to him my true feelings of fear and horror at the thought of marriage, he was amazed at my violence, but unconvinced that any female could verily desire to remain unwed.

All too soon there arose the matter of the wretched Catherine Grey. The girl must have had a maggot in her brain, for sure. The first inkling I had of the whole sorry business was when Robert sought an interview with me one morning while we were at Ipswich. He came in, frowning and looking perplexed. I was alone, lounging upon a cushioned settle, setting some words to music.

'A merry morning to you, Rob. How is it

with you, my dearest?'

'I am greatly worried, Elizabeth. A matter has been confided to me that is too weighty for my mind, and surely one that you should know of.'

'Indeed?' I enquired lazily, smiling up at him and taking deep pleasure in his handsome looks. 'Sit ye and tell of it then.'

'You will not like it,' he said.

'Come, Rob, out with it. What is this weighty matter and who told you of it?'

He shrugged his shoulders. 'The Lady Catherine Grey,' he replied.

'Lady Catherine? What could she have to tell you? And why you?'

'God knows, unless she feels that I have some kin to her through her sister's marriage with my brother Guildford.'

'Well, what is it?'

'My Queen, she is married — '

'Married!' I shouted, jerking myself upright. 'Married without my consent? When did she tell you this?'

'Last night.'

'Last night, Rob? You were with me until we retired.'

He coughed. 'She visited me in my bedchamber,' he said, with an air of embarrassment that would have been comical had I not been so overstruck.

I leaped up, papers and music falling to the floor in a cascade of sheets. 'What is she to you, Rob?' I asked, dead quiet.

Up he sprang in his turn, seizing me by the shoulders. 'Nay, nay, she is nothing,' he reassured me. 'Would I have told you else?' I saw the force of that and besought him to continue. 'Well, then,' he went on, 'I was asleep when she appeared like some tearful wraith at my bedside, imploring my help. I give you my word, I near died of shock. For a moment, I thought 'twas her sister's ghost come — '

'Never mind that,' I interrupted ruthlessly, 'go on. What next?'

'She told me she was married, but that none knew of it. *'Who is your husband?'* I whispered. *''Tis the Lord Hertford,'* says she.'

'Good God,' I said, sitting down with a thump. 'He is in France and has been for some months.'

'Ay indeed,' agreed Rob. ' *'Who brought all this to pass?'* says I to her. *'Oh, the Lady Jane Seymour arranged it all,'* sobs Lady Catherine. *'Now she is dead and I am pregnant'.*'

'Pregnant!' I screeched. 'Oh, it is too much! And to think of Lady Jane Seymour going secretly behind my back to engineer this. How false! Why, I gave her an expensive funeral! Nay, do not laugh, Rob. 'Twas a sneaking thing to do. I'll wager she thought marriage with my heir would be a fine thing for her beggarly brother! Well, it shall not work so, I promise you.'

His smile faded. 'I was afire with anxiety lest she had been seen entering or leaving my chamber, and the matter repeated to you before I could tell you of it,' he explained.

'Has she proof of the marriage?' I asked. 'That clergyman who wed them will regret it.'

Rob shook his head. 'She has no proof. She knew not the minister's name, and Lady Jane who was sole witness, is dead.'

I turned up my eyes to Heaven and wrung my fingers together in an access of exasperation. 'Go on, give me the whole,' I said flatly.

'Then she said that before he left for France, Lord Hertford gave her a deed of jointure worth £1,000 a year.'

'Humph!' I snorted. 'A goodly sum. Would I had known he had so much to waste! Where is the deed now?'

'She has lost it.'

'Lost it!' I was scarce able to believe my ears. 'Lost the sole proof to her marriage? Is the girl half-witted?'

'I do not know her well enough to say,' replied Rob virtuously. 'But she is in a rare taking, for she has had no word from Lord Hertford since he left. She assured me that she sought my help only as a last resort, having asked advice of Lady Saintlow but just before. She would have none of it, not wishing the responsibility, and sent the girl away. So Lady Catherine came to me.'

'Lady Saintlow,' I repeated. 'Just so. The longest and busiest tongue in the land. She could not have chosen a worse confidante. The girl has no sense, no judgment, and she is to carry on the Succession. God help England, I say, if aught should happen to me and its ruling were left to her. Of course, there is always my cousin of Scotland to fall back on, I suppose, and I tremble to imagine the disasters *she* would bring in her train! Find that idiot girl, Rob, and send her straight to me.'

While I waited for Lady Catherine, to my amazement I began to weep. My stomach churned with envy and frustration, also with fury at her slyness and defiance of me. Striving to control myself, I walked about the room, screwing up my eyes to quell the tears, compressing my lips to still their trembling, holding my breath to check the sobs that rose in my throat. I was almost twenty-seven, near unto thirty, and never, never would I know what she knew — the feel of a babe in my womb, nor marriage, however secret, to the man I loved. Upon these agonising reflections, the door opened to admit Lady Catherine. She stood just inside the doorway, her back to the wall, staring at me in a mixture of fear and defiance. I stared back, the tears still in my eyes. In silence she curtsied. I looked her up and down, from the top of her bright red head of Tudor hair to the tips of her blue embroidered slippers.

'Well,' I said hardly, 'what have you to say for yourself?'

She swallowed, her pale face flushing. 'Madam, I am not ashamed of what I did.'

'No? Then why did we all not share your joy? Why such secrecy, Lady Catherine?'

'I — I thought you would not consent,' she faltered.

'You were right. I should not have done so.'

'Why not? Do you grudge me happiness?'

'Insolent!' I cried. 'How dare you bandy words with me! I have shown you interest and favour as my legal heir. I am your Sovereign, Lady Catherine, and in your position it is obligatory that the matter of your marriage should be discussed most carefully. You have a responsibility to England and to me. Yet you go behind my back, you connive, you lie! Have you aught to say?'

She tossed her head. 'My husband is of good blood.'

I snorted. 'Of cold blood, too, it seems, if he has sent you no message. A wild, desirous lover indeed. I hear you have no knowledge of the cleric who wed you, and that you have lost this precious deed of jointure left you by your so-called husband.'

'He is truly my husband!' she cried.

'Dear me, you are wondrous defiant,' I remarked acidly. 'And to think I put down your sad looks to the fact that you have been mourning Lady Jane Seymour!'

'Oh, I do mourn her, indeed I do!'

'I'll warrant you do,' I said unpleasantly, 'she having been your only witness in this disgraceful hole-and-corner affair. How do I know that what you carry is not a bastard? You cannot prove it, can you? Do you not understand, girl? As my heiress-presumptive, the child you are to bear is third in Succession to the throne of England — should it be legitimate, that is!'

'It is legitimate! You insult me! You think that because you are Queen, you can ride roughshod — '

I dealt her a ringing slap on the cheek that

effectually silenced her. 'On your knees!' I shouted. 'Down on your knees, you insolent bitch to speak so to me, your Queen! You have done wrong, you have demeaned your high position of trust and honour, and you dare dispute with me! By God, you shall learn different!' I glared down at her kneeling before me, tiny and white-faced, with the red mark of my hand upon her cheek. Nowhere near as pretty as her sister Jane had been, but full as irritating. I restrained the desire to give her a sharp kick, and clenched my toes in their velvet shoon.

'I shall recall this purported husband of yours,' I said, 'and he shall join you in the residence I have planned for you.' A small triumphant smile quivered at the corner of her mouth and her sandy-fringed lids dropped, veiling her eyes. In the blue wrapper she wore, the bulge of her pregnancy could clearly be seen. 'Yes,' I went on smoothly, 'he shall join you. In the Tower. You shall be escorted there this very day. I cannot promise that you will actually meet your laggard spouse there, but rest assured that he will at least be under the same roof as yourself e'er long.'

Her mouth dropped open and she caught her breath with shock and dismay. 'Oh no!' she gasped. 'Oh no, cousin! Do not send me there. Oh, you cannot!'

' 'Cannot' is no word to use to me, Lady Catherine,' I rapped out. 'I both can and will. Now go before I lose the remains of my temper. Leave me.'

She caught my ankles. 'But I loved him so dear! You must understand. Do you not know what love is? Have you no heart?'

I drew a deep breath at this. 'Not know love?' I hissed at her through set teeth. 'Not know love? You fool, you have no wit, no sense, no insight — nay, you are no more fit to follow me than is a worm — a slug! Oh, I know love full well, Catherine Grey, and bitter sorrow it gives me. But I cannot marry where I will, and I will not marry where I can. I cannot afford to let my heart rule my head and give up all for what men call love!'

She threw up her head and shrieked at me. 'Nay, *you* cannot, nor will you let anyone else! You are greedy, cruel and jealous! Jealous! Jealous!' It was as if a weasel had roared.

'Out!' I bellowed. 'Get out, you fleering, white-faced cat! Be ready to leave Ipswich immediately after noonday, or matters will go worse with you yet! Get out!' She stumbled to her feet and made for the door. I speeded her going with a comfit box, a fan, a wooden dish, a cushion and a book of music. Then, when she had gone, I laid my head upon the table and broke into such a passion of tears that I gave myself a blinding headache and could eat naught, nor be comfortable for the rest of the day. Catherine Grey had spoken truth. Jealous indeed I was. Vilely, cruelly, wickedly, woundingly jealous, wounding myself as well as her. Mayhap it was also true that I knew not the meaning of love. I could not bear such truth; I could not bear the girl near me. She had touched a raw place too close.

Apart from all this, I could not condone her conduct, for by all that was held to be right and good in our times, a sovereign must have some disposal in the marriage of an heir. I could not be seen to have allowed such behaviour in her, so irresponsible and silly as she was. Yet what better choice had I? Why, a child of my own body. So, with one swing, I was straight back to the vexed and frightening question of my own marriage.

My ministers fretted over the problem day and night. There was no other but I, Elizabeth Tudor, with the ability to rule this country and bring her back to peace and greatness. If I should die, what then? Chaos for sure, and death for many. So

Elizabeth Tudor must wed and have children to provide for the Succession, and pray to God that they inherit her powers.

But Elizabeth Tudor would not, for she could not. It was beyond her spirit and her strength. It was a rock against which will and reason foundered.

Once Lady Catherine had left Ipswich, my anger and distress abated somewhat. I intended her no hardship in the Tower. She should have comfortable apartments, her ladies to attend her and time to reflect upon her thoughtless actions. I would not allow her to cohabit with her husband, if so he was. I needed to discover more about the business from him and to give him time to think, also. I wished him to realise that what he had done was mighty near to treason. In time I would release them, but not before I was satisfied as to their future behaviour.

There was yet more to fidget me that August, and over another cousin. Cecil had suggested to me that Marie Stuart should give up any claim to the English throne if I would recognise her as my heiress-presumptive, to succeed me if I had no children. I could not agree to this. Also, Marie had refused to ratify the Treaty of Edinburgh, drawn up so painfully the previous year, so I had no compunction at all in refusing her request for a safe-conduct upon her journey to Scotland.

'Let her make her own safe-conduct!' I said sharply to Cecil. 'No doubt her Catholic saints will protect her, for I shall not!'

But I relented and sent her a safe-conduct after all, for upon deeper thought, I realised that we should both have much to gain if I met her, discussed the terms of an agreement, and sent her on her way through England with my blessing. Unluckily, she was too precipitate, or I had lingered too long, for she had already taken ship for Scotland by the time my safe-conduct arrived in France. She landed at Leith on 19th August 1561 in a haar, which is the word they use there for a certain thick, wet, dark fog.

An inauspicious beginning, I felt, and my thought was shared by the Protestant preacher John Knox, who said that the fog showed what she brought with her, namely, 'sorrow, darkness and all impiety.' A saucy, insolent fellow he, a humourless fanatic without a gleam of humanity or ease in his nature. He had already writ a presumptuous book entitled: *The First Blast of the Trumpet Against the Monstrous Regiment of Women* a few months before I came to my throne. As far as I was concerned, his first blast would remain his last. Marie was not to be so fortunate as I. Knox was her countryman, her subject and a red-hot Protestant, destined to make life uncomfortable for her, and in this he did his best, being a very thorn in her flesh from first to last.

I was much annoyed that we had missed the chance to meet. This mis-timing showed our divergent natures very clearly. I would always tarry and draw things out until the pieces fell together or until I saw which way matters were leaning, while she, wildly impulsive, would never wait and watch, but act first, be it right or wrong. So she was to rush upon her doom, in spite of all.

All things considered, I was glad when the time came to return home, for in spite of the loyal and loving welcome of my people, I had not enjoyed this Progress. The weather had been poor and there had been much to fret my already irritated nerves. Even our leaving was attended by annoyance, for the day was pouring wet and the ways out of East Anglia were like a succession of quagmires. It was a fitting end to a cross and uncomfortable Progress, and we made all speed for fair Placentia lying upon its sweet curve of the Thames at Greenwich.

Whilst there, I thought it politic to receive the Grand Prior and the Constable of France upon their return from escorting Queen Marie to Scotland. Although Marie had not got my safe-conduct, I did not wish to offend her influential relative, the Grand Prior, nor his equally powerful companion, by churlish neglect of the respect due to their position. Therefore, I decided upon a goodly banquet and entertainment to show them that the English Queen might be as rich and powerful as themselves.

I devised a ballet depicting the tale of the Wise and Foolish Virgins to amuse my august visitors, and to mark the day of my birth, also. It turned out very well, being held in the Great Chamber just as dusk was falling and a clear golden light illumining the room, the shadows growing deeper every moment. At the end of the dance, I entered through green velvet hangings against which I stood poised. I was rewarded by the drawn breath of admiration from my audience which came plain to my ears. I looked very well indeed, being attired all in white and silver, my red hair loose to proclaim my own virginity. Twined in my hair were pearls and diamonds, and round my neck, ropes of pearls and diamonds falling near to my knees. Again I blessed my father and dear

Queen Catherine Parr for the jewels they had left me, enabling me to make a brave show upon many a needful occasion such as this. My guests were impressed and full of compliments, seeming happy to be pleased, so the result was worth the effort.

* * *

The news, but three weeks later, that Catherine Grey had been brought to bed, in the Tower, of a son called Edward, on the 24th of September did little to delight me, for here was another claimant too close for comfort, and a boy at that. I thought that this match must be the beginning of a scheme to bring the Greys and Seymours forward, to my detriment and consequent ill-fortune of the realm. I decided, therefore, that mother and son should remain in the Tower, apart from so-called husband and father also held therein, until I could enquire more closely into the validity of this marriage. Cecil thought me too harsh and said so, assuring me that he knew of no conspiracy, but I could not be easy about it.

I kept Mary Grey, the youngest sister of Jane and Catherine, near me at Court as a Maid-of-Honour, to be under my eye and thus hindered from any misdemeanour or misalliance such as her sister had made. The girl was, after all, a relative, an orphan in need of protection. I did not anticipate any naughtiness from her, she being so plain and seemingly afraid of her own shadow. She was almost dwarfish, with a hunched shoulder due to some birth injury, and a head of frizzy carroty hair. I doubted that any man would make a fool of himself for her sake, much less marry her clandestinely.

I could not like any of that family. It seemed strange that my beautiful aunt Mary Rose, my father's young and much-loved sister, should have bred such an unlovable and luckless dynasty. I felt it sad that so many of my Tudor relatives should be such a charge on me. Even my aunt Margaret Tudor, elder sister to my father, had been grandmother to my worrisome cousin Marie Stuart and had borne for daughter the detestable Margaret Lennox who hated me. Nay, I was not fortunate in the Tudor side of my family; I preferred my mother's relatives by far, finding them warm, witty, lovable and kind for the most part, asking but little from me and so receiving the more.

William Maitland of Lethington, Secretary of State for Scotland, travelled down to see me at this time, and I recall that I railed to him of Catherine Grey and her child, saying that I felt very deeply about the business.

'By having a child and being in the Succession, she has declared to the world that she would be more worthy of a throne than your Queen or myself, who have none. It riles me, Maitland.' He nodded sympathetically, and I went on: 'Now, about the Succession itself. We must talk of this, for it is a matter that concerns us all.'

Lethington assured me of Queen Marie's goodwill and of her longing to meet me. I returned the sentiment, adding that she had a greater right to inherit than the Greys, she being descended from my father's elder sister. But there were conditions to her becoming my heir, I said. I wished her to have no league with France, to have and foster friendship with England in herself and her country. I wished her to marry acceptably, and in time, convert to the Protestant faith. Lethington looked dubious at this, but suggested that these difficulties might well be resolved if she and I could meet.

Before he returned to Scotland, I charged Lethington to keep in correspondence with Cecil, and sent with him Sir Peter Mewtas to offer Marie an official welcome. In truth, Sir Peter was to demand the ratification of the Treaty of Edinburgh as well as to deliver his more polite message. My cousin sent a letter to me, in answer, suggesting that the whole matter be reviewed afresh in charge of new Commissioners. I would not agreed to this, preferring it to be done by Tom Randolph, my Ambassador in Scotland, whom I could trust.

Her answer to me was full of conciliatory charm, which I found right pleasing. Truly I would have liked to have seen her, and when I replied to her letter, I did not refuse a meeting, nor yet did I agree; it was not my way to be too positive over matters of great moment. But I enjoyed her notes and missives. She sent me verses, and later, a fair ring with a diamond in it shaped like a heart, the ring enclosed in more verses, these in French and very pretty. So upon one of Randolph's journeys to the North, he carried from me a fine and handsome ring from me to her, which, I heard, she marvellously esteemed and many times kissed.

'Indeed,' Tom Randolph told me, 'the Scottish Queen wishes that one of the two were a man, thus to make an end of all debates. This, I trow,' he added drily, and looking primly upon me, 'was spoken in her merry mood.'

'And well spoken,' I laughed, 'for 'tis truth. It would surely settle all.'

During the latter part of the year I tasted the sweets of revenge; a mild enough revenge as it turned out, but very satisfactory for all that. Since I had come to the throne resolving to be generous, I had received my hateful cousin Margaret Douglas of Lennox at my Court and had accorded her the full precedence that was her due there. This lady had been right spiteful and malicious to me in my young days of danger, causing much bitterness between me and my sister by her lies and insults. While at my Court, she strained my magnanimity near to breaking point by her air of condescension towards me, giving me the merest deference, her hostility and jealousy barely covered by the thinnest skin of surface politeness. I was glad that she elected to spend most of her time in Yorkshire at her family home of Temple Newsam, for if she had stayed at Court, I verily believe we would have come to blows between us.

Needless to say, Temple Newsam was a gathering point for discontented Catholics and a hotbed of malice against me. At last, this grew too much for a servant of the household, who, having a grudge against the Lennoxes, saw a way to vent his spleen, gain favour and a better place, all in one venture. He came to London to seek audience of me, and I saw the fellow, listening to what he had to say. A big rustic, with a bandaged head, he knelt awestruck on the rushes before me, at first seemingly dumb-struck also. I asked him if he had news for me from my cousin's home, bidding him to speak up without fear.

At last he nodded portentously. 'Ay, Queen,' he said solemnly, 'they talk agin you oop there, and they treated I bad.' He pointed to the bandage. 'Cracked I over the 'ed, my Lord did. Threw I out, my Lady did, and I wi' a wife an' little 'uns. So I be angered. I'll show 'en, says I. And I coom to you, Queen.'

'I see. And what said they against me?'

'Why, Lady, to make a rising 'gainst you. And, save your Honour, 'twas 'That fool bastard,' they called you, and 'The Horsemaster's Mistress.' I heard 'en.'

'Very pretty, i'faith. Is there more?'

'Ay, Lady. My mistress has a son called Lord Darnley. She says as he would make a foine 'usband for the Queen of Scotland. She says as good Cartholics maun band together to make him so.'

'Most interesting,' I agreed. 'You have been useful, fellow. I will see that you are suitably rewarded. Go now, my people will look after you.'

This was but one of the many reports I had received of the doings at Temple Newsam. I knew, too, that Lady Lennox had been intriguing with De Quadra to put forward her son as a candidate for Queen Marie's hand. It was enough. I decided to put a spoke in their conspiratorial wheel and invited the Lennoxes, with the Earls of Northumberland and Westmorland, both involved with the Lennoxes, to spend the days of Christmas with me at Court. As my invitation was more in the nature of a command, they came promptly, if slightly puzzled at my seeming affability. It was not long before I took issue with Lady Margaret.

I summoned her to my private cabinet, where I was playing cards with Ann Russell and Katey, the table pulled close to the fire for warmth. In flounced my Lady, sketching me the barest curtsey, her eyes full of indignant enquiry. I kept her standing while we finished the game, deaf to her sighs and foot-tappings. At last I laid down the cards. 'Now, my dear cousin,' said I, velvet-smooth, 'what is all this I have been hearing about you?'

She tossed her head. 'I have no idea what your Majesty may mean,' she answered, raising her brows insolently.

'Come, come, Lady Margaret,' I purred,

'have you not been busy at Temple Newsam? Have you not had many Catholic visitors there, full of plots and plans?'

'They are but friends!' she flashed. 'I know not what you mean by plots, cousin.'

'No? Then you will not mind leaving your friends for a while. I would have you nearer me. Blood is thicker than water, so they say.'

'I pray you, do not speak me in riddles, Madam. I have no wit for puzzles.'

'It seems that you consider me to suffer the same infirmity,' I replied, 'for I would like an explanation of your words with De Quadra upon the subject of your son and the Queen of Scots.'

'As to that,' she answered hotly, 'I have every right to make such a match for my son. Queen Marie is my close relative by blood, through my mother's first marriage, and made closer still by mine own marriage to Matthew Stuart of Lennox. I wish to wed my son to her, for so may the Succession be secured to Queen Marie, and thus all reason for strife be avoided if you yourself die without issue.'

Ah, the interfering, wrong-headed bitch! I felt a tide of anger rising in me, but checked it, for I wished not to give her the satisfaction of making me lose my temper. 'Highly

165

laudable,' said I. 'I admire your concern for the future of the realm. However, I consider that to be *my* business, cousin, as I consider the marriage of an heir my business also. As well as this, although you may feel you have the right to make a match for your son in this way, I fear you are sadly mistaken. To enter into a matter that touches the Sovereign so nearly, you need her permission. You have not asked it.'

'Nay, indeed,' she cried haughtily, 'and why should I?'

'Take care, Madam,' I warned. 'You forget yourself. Where is your son, Lord Darnley, at present?'

'He is in France,' she snapped.

'Indeed? Visiting the Guise family, I presume, with a view to further his suit for Queen Marie's hand? Do not trouble to affirm or deny it, cousin, I know it to be true. I know a great deal.'

'Ah, you are jealous!' she burst out. 'Jealous that I have a son — '

'The boot is on the other foot,' I cut in. 'I would say that you are jealous of me.' She flushed and bridled angrily. 'Now, Lady Margaret,' I went on, 'I have recalled a most important and significant thing to do with the marriage of your parents. Surely your mother's marriage to your father was annulled? Pray correct me if I am wrong, cousin. It seems to me that if a marriage be annulled it be no marriage, nor never has been. In which case, my dear, *you* are illegitimate, and your offspring have no importance whatever as possible heirs.'

Jesu, but I thought she would have an apoplexy. Her face grew purple, she gurgled and stuttered on broken words of rage and protest. Sure, it was a sweet moment. I revelled in it for a short space, then spoke again. 'See now, Lady Lennox, you must have time and peace in which to consider your new status. I suggest that you take up residence with Sir Richard Sackville at Sheen. He will watch over you well, for my sake, while you are there. The Earl Matthew, your husband, will lodge in the Tower for a time.'

'You cannot do this!' she cried. 'I say you cannot!'

'Cannot?' I queried silkily. 'Dear me, cousin, have you again forgotten that 'The Horsemaster's Mistress' — or was it 'That fool bastard' — is Queen, with absolute power of life and death over you, her subject? Ah, I see you recall those less than complimentary words used, at your home, to describe me. Well, see that you forget not again the rank of her to whom they were applied, my Lady.

167

You will have ample time to remember it at Sheen. Now go.'

When she had backed out of the room, all amazed with confusion and dismay, I smiled at Ann and Katey, who, knowing the state of affairs between the Lennoxes and me, had savoured every word of this interview. 'Tit for tat,' said I, picking up the cards. 'Come, deal me again.'

★ ★ ★

In France, in early January, was issued the Edict of St. Germains. I discussed it with Cecil at Hampton Court. By this edict, the French Protestants, or Huguenots, as they were called, had been granted religious tolerance, even near self-government in some special towns and places. On the surface it seemed fair enough, but in reality was useless, for the power-hungry Catholic Guise family would resist it with all their might, even to bloodshed. Moreover, Paris itself was as Catholic as my London was Protestant. The business could not go smoothly.

'Mark me, Cecil,' I said, 'it will be but a week or two before we hear of murders and killings. I hope it will not upset my Catholic peers in the North and so cause trouble in England. This edict has been put forward at

168

the wrong time. France is not ready for it.'

Sure enough, in the very same month, the Guise faction seized Paris and scenes of horrid violence erupted, culminating on the first of March in the massacre of more than a thousand souls at Vassy. Cecil sought audience of me while the breezes were playing their music in Richmond's spires. I decided to send a large party into Yorkshire, ostensibly as a hunting expedition, including in it my cousin Henry Carey Earl of Hunsdon, the Duke of Norfolk, and the Earls of Northampton, Rutland and Huntingdon — powerful nobles all. I fancied that this band would prove an effective deterrent to any lordly Northern hothead who might have caught the seeds of disaffection from France. And it did, for the North remained peaceful.

In April, my good Ambassador Throckmorton wrote from France that civil war was brewing, and now was the time to make a push to recover Calais, if I wanted it, or if not Calais, some useful port on the French coast. This idea appealed to me, for, in my eyes, as well as those of my countrymen, Calais was still English, having been so for hundreds of years until lost in my sister's unhappy reign. It would be good indeed to recover it, and I sent Sir Henry Sidney to

Paris to talk terms, for I would always sooner gain my ends through peaceful methods, if possible.

Unluckily, peaceful methods did not prevail, and because fighting was now breaking out all over France, there was actual danger that the Catholic cause might triumph. Cecil was in deepest gloom over the whole affair, and wrought upon me so much that I attended the next full Council meeting in person. During this meeting it was decided to man the fleet and hold in readiness for sailing to Normandy if the situation worsened. Afterwards, Cecil gave me a memorandum that he had drawn up for me, begging me to give it my full attention. I took it to my cabinet, and a doom-laden counsel of woe I found it. Sitting glumly, chin on hand, I pondered it, staring absently into space the while. There came a scratching on the door and I heard Rob's voice. I called to him to come in and cheer me, for I was in a doleful dump. In he came, smiling, asking what ailed me.

'Why, 'tis this from Cecil,' I said. 'He writes that if the Protestants should lose this struggle, Spain will take Navarre, the Guises will put Marie upon my throne, she will wed Prince Carlos of Spain, and the Spaniards will take Ireland. Is that not enough to cause an attack of melancholy?'

'Well, but he is right. We should interfere, my love, and with all speed. It is a serious matter.'

'Ay, but I will not have it is as dire as Cecil says. Nor am I as rash and hot-headed as you,' I said, dropping a kiss on that same hot head. With that, he reached up pulling me down to him and we forgot France for a space.

Nevertheless, I was right concerned about the foreign situation and also much beset by the constant urging of my Councillors for me to wed. To withstand them stretched my tricky nerves to snapping point. Also, there had been a long and minute enquiry into Catherine Grey's marriage, which I had to keep, in all detail, in the forefront of my mind, devilish nuisance that it was. After a deal of talk, the marriage was declared invalid and Edward Seymour brought before the Court of the Star Chamber. Here he was fined £15,000 for seducing a virgin of the Blood Royal, for virgin she had been, having never bedded with Lord Pembroke's son in her previous marriage.

Once this was over, I felt I could breathe fairly easy for a while. I intended to release Catherine, and Edward Seymour too, once their hot blood had cooled, and I would have kept an eye on the silly girl's son, for after all, he was kin of mine. How was I to guess that she and her disallowed husband would continue to meet and bed together, there in the Tower, defying all? Now that I am old and have more of understanding, I see that they must have truly loved, poor things, and I know also that I feel much pity and regret, for hard indeed I was upon them. Cecil told me so often enough, but I could not listen, for it was all bound up in my inmost self with my own so-called bastardy, my own insecurity, humiliation, fear of sex and death. Moreover, my Queenship was growing ever more upon me, and soft and sentimental I could not be. Never was I inclined that way, and what little I possessed was soon rooted out by the exigencies of my great and responsible position. Sympathy oft I felt, but those two needed more than mere sympathy in their pathos and bewilderment. What they needed was not in me to give. Mayhap I was neither clear-sighted nor clear-headed about the wretched Catherine Grey; I could not be, struggle with myself as I would.

Nor could I be about marriage; mine own or anyone else's. It was all too near to my deepest, secret fears. Yea, I will be judged hard, I will be judged cruel, spiteful and mean. So I was, so I am. 'Tis all part o' me. Yet never, never have I abased myself to gain love. I have never loved easy, neither, but those I have loved I have loved all my life. True to mine own spirit have I ever been and reaped a great reward thereby, for spite of my hardness, my unkindnesses, my parsimoniousness, my autocratic temper, still am I spoke of as Blessed, as Goddess, Heart of Men's Desire, Saviour of England.

5

FROM DEATH TO LIFE RECOVERED

August 1562 to December 1562

On the first of August I had a secret meeting with the Vidâme de Chartres, a Huguenot minister who commanded Le Havre, in order to discuss terms of English intervention in the French uproar. After six weeks a treaty was concluded, in which it was settled that Le Havre was to be delivered to an English garrison, and then, in return for gold and mercantile support, exchanged for Calais. It was a wild venture, and wild I must have been to agree to it.

At the beginning of October, Ambrose Lord Warwick, Rob's elder brother, took command of the military expedition, and upon the fifth of the month, he took Le Havre. I could not approve of the sort of men he had in his command. They were short-sighted hot-heads for the most part, who had been active in the Wyatt conspiracy during my sister's reign. I could not truly trust these men to remain calm with swords in their hands and a fight in the offing; they were not well-known for their circumspection. They viewed the whole enterprise in the light of an exciting prank, and not as the secret political move I would have it. Of course, I had listened too much to Rob and had allowed myself to be carried too far upon the tide of his enthusiasm, but allow him to command the expedition I would not. I wished him alive. Indeed, I felt uneasy about the whole business, sensing in my bones that it could come to no good. Nor did it, as I was later to discover.

I had moved the Court to Hampton for the autumn of that year, hoping to find some peace from the nervous fret that had plagued me for several months, yet I felt but little recovered, having much on my mind. I was easily tired and snappish, suffering from headaches and bouts of tears. One morning I awoke feeling worse than usual, with a wambling belly, heavy eyes, a pain in the head and a dull discomfort in all my limbs. I decided to ride, to clear away this sluggish humour, but returned after a short while, chilled rather than warmed by the exercise. To the dismay of my ladies, I announced that I would have a bath, so refusing all advice, I had the bath filled in my bathing room. It was good and comforting, causing me to feel refreshed and nigh recovered from my malaise. When Kat bade me rest I said I would ride in the park, for I was recovered, and so I remained. But not so the next day, nor the day after that. Indeed, when Cecil came to me to discuss a letter to be written to Queen Marie, 'twas all I could do to keep my mind on the matter. I was sitting hunched over the fire in my private parlour, huddled in a fur-lined robe, when Cecil craved admittance.

'Come in,' I said wearily. 'God's nails, but I am low today. What would you, Cecil?'

He bowed. 'Madam, 'tis of Lord Warwick's force in France — ' he began.

'Oh, sit you,' I interrupted fretfully, waving him to a stool nearby. 'I tell you, I would we had kept out of France altogether. It has been a plaguey business from the start. What of it?'

'Should we not send some sort of communication to the Scottish Queen to acquaint her of the reason for our garrison at Le Havre? After all, she is kin to the Guises.'

'Cecil, my wits must be wandering. To tell truth, I feel not so sprightly today. Of course a letter must be sent.'

'Ay, Madam. I had thought it might be best to emphasise that our men are there not to make war, but merely to stay the worst cruelties against the Huguenots, and mayhap keep a port or two open for our trading ships.'

'Oh admirable indeed. And if, by chance, our soldiers should, in the general melée, *happen* to take Calais, very well and good! Just so. I will write the Queen a letter now. I will oil and butter it well, never fear. Pass me my father's desk; I will have it on my knee, for I care not to move from the fire. I feel wretched, Cecil.'

'Does your Majesty then mislike the whole scheme so greatly?'

'Oh I mislike it very greatly. I have allowed myself to be over-persuaded in the conducting of it, that I know. I know also that never will I do so again. My own judgment is best; always was and always will be.' He nodded in agreement and I went on: 'The thing is, I feel unwell, but do not fret. I daresay it is naught.'

He passed me the little desk, looking somewhat concerned. I took it from him and set it upon my knee. Full oft had I seen my father use this desk. I lifted the lid and ran my hand fondly over the green leather writing surface thus revealed, raising one of the decorated lids, searching for a pen. 'Sweet Christ!' I said pettishly. ' 'Tis too heavy for my knees. Fetch a table, Cecil, I will have it on a table by the fire. God, but I am cold! Dost think I am stewing a rheum?'

'I pray not, dear Madam,' he answered, worried. ''Tis better you leave the letter until tomorrow.' But I said I would do it now, whilst it was in my mind, and he asked solicitously: 'Will you take a posset, or rest abed, Madam? Autumn is a chancy time for agues and fevers. You must take care, so precious you are to us.'

I smiled at him and bade him leave me to my writing. In truth, I felt quite ill, and now that he had gone, realised that no longer did I feel cold but mighty warm; warm as if afire. Cecil was right, I had an autumn fever, pest take it. Cursing my bad luck, I began my letter, telling Queen Marie that English interference in France was necessary only to keep the French channel ports open to English trading ships and to attempt to check the cruelties used against the Huguenots. It was a good letter; diplomatic, friendly and very reasonable, but my head ached so fiercely that I could write no longer. I flexed my fingers, cramped from holding the quill. They were slippery with sweat. Seizing the pen again, I scribbled: 'My hot fever prevents me writing more,' and cast the pen aside.

'Katey!' I called. 'Cousin Katey!' I rang my little handbell impatiently and my cousin Knollys came hurrying to me from my bed-chamber. 'Katey,' I said, 'shake the sand castor over this letter and put it in my desk. I can do no more, my dear. I fear I have caught a little fever.' Looking alarmed, she begged me to leave the letter, but I insisted she do my bidding. Then I asked her to find Kat Ashley. 'Send her to me,' I gasped. 'She will know how to ease me.'

In the event, it turned out that none knew how to ease me, not even my Kat. I was truly ill, and my fever mounted steadily, causing me the greatest discomfort and pain. At last it was decided to call a doctor and after a great discussion amongst my relatives fussing about my bed, they hit upon one Dr. Burcot, a German physician. He had treated my cousin Henry Carey with much success, and both my cousins seemed to think excellent well of him.

'Well, call him then!' I groaned. 'Body of God, I feel as if my last hour is upon me.'

At this, they flew into such a taking that had I not been so grievous sick, I would have laughed. Very soon the doctor arrived; a square-faced, square-headed, square-bodied earnest fellow, who looked at my tongue, my eyes, my back, chest, arms, in my ears, down my throat, until all the secrets of my illness must be revealed I thought. 'Come, man, what is it? What have I got?' I croaked as he walked to the window and stood staring out over the privy garden. 'Do not haver with me. I will know.'

At last he swung round, the light from the windows at his back so that my aching, watering eyes could not see his face clearly. Suddenly he burst out: 'My liege, thou shalt have the pox!'

'What!' I screamed, struggling to raise myself in the bed. 'Rogue, villain, dolt, what sayest thou?' Such a noise I made that my people came running, all aghast. 'Have the knave away out of my sight!' I screeched. 'Send him hence! Out, out, I say!'

They bundled him out forthwith, while I tossed and turned with mounting fever. So the days passed and I grew worse, but no spots appeared upon me, yet my fever raged so violent that I could not finish my letter to Scotland, nor even raise myself on my pillows. Dear Mary Sidney proved a wondrous nurse, Kat irritating me near to craziness by her weeping and fretting. My own doctors could do naught for me and at last they sent for Cecil, telling him that I was to die. He, in a state of terror at his secret dread like to come true, called a meeting of the Privy Council to discuss the matter of the Succession, but I was unconscious and knew naught of this until some weeks later.

There was no one fit to take my place and they knew it. Catherine Grey, her cousin Margaret Strange, or Lord Huntingdon who sprang from the old Plantagenet stock, were the only names that Cecil and the Council would even consider. Marie of Scotland was never spoken of, for to have her would be out of the question and ruin all that had been achieved. Yet they must be quick to decide before the King of Spain could meddle and thus cause an equal disaster.

Coming round from my swoon, I saw Cecil and all the members of the Council standing round my bed, all in tears. I heard my ladies sobbing. *Christ*, thought I, *I am dying and they are here to see me go. I must do somewhat for Rob, quick, quick* . . . So I forced myself to speak.

'My lords,' I whispered so low that they had to bend down to hear me, 'I desire you to appoint Lord Robert Dudley . . .'

'Ay, my liege, what then?' asked Cecil gently, as I paused to gasp for breath.

'Lord Robert is to be Protector of the Realm . . .' I went on painfully, ' . . . with payment of £20,000 a year . . . Then there is Tamworth . . . his body-servant . . . Thou knowest Tamworth, Cecil? He sleeps in Rob's room ... He must have £500 a year ... See to it, I charge you ... I charge you.'

'Is there aught else, Madam?' asked Cecil.

'Ay. Prithee be good to ... my dear cousin ... Henry Carey Lord Hunsdon ... and all my people and servants.'

'We will, we will!' they assured me, their voices all broken with sobs and tears.

'And now I call upon God Himself ... to witness that although ... I love, and have always loved ... Lord Robert most dearly ... nothing improper ... has ever passed ... between us.'

'Amen and amen,' they murmured soothingly.

While all this was going on, two messengers, riding with a third horse between them, had gone with all speed to Dr. Burcot's house to fetch him back to me, to save my life if he could. He would not come at first, so I heard later. He had been mortal offended in his professional pride by my fearful and angry words five days earlier.

'By God's pestilence!' he had shouted hardily. 'If she be sick, let her die! Called me a knave, she did, for my goodwill! Nay, I stay here, and so tell her!'

One of the messengers, servant to the Carey family, grabbed the doctor's cloak and boots, drew his dagger menacingly and roared at the doctor that if he did not dress and go with them at once, he would be stabbed to death then and there. So, forcing his feet into the boots, snatching the cloak and bawling terrible German oaths, Dr. Burcot rushed down the stairs, leaped upon the extra horse and pounded away in the direction of Hampton, the relieved messengers galloping behind.

When he came to my bedside, he barked ferociously: 'Almost too late, my liege!' and began to rap out orders to my people, who flew to obey. A mattress was put down on the floor before the fire, then I was wrapped from head to foot in a length of scarlet cloth, leaving but one hand free. I was carried to the mattress and laid upon it, everything about me swimming before my fevered eyes. Kneeling beside me, he raised my head, put a bottle to my lips and bade me drink all or any of it as I wished. It was very comfortable, and I told him so in a cracked whisper, taking the bottle in my free hand and drinking greedily. After a space, I noticed red spots appearing upon that hand, and cried out, all afraid: 'Oh, what is this, Master Doctor? See my hand, see my hand!'

'I told you, 'tis the pox,' said he impatiently.

Loud did I wail and lament, but fierce Dr. Burcot would have none of that. 'God's pestilence!' he bellowed. 'Which is better? To have the pox in the face and in the hands, or in the heart and kill the whole body?'

I said no more, but sobbed quietly to myself, for I was weak and very sick. He was right, I knew, but at that moment I felt I would rather die than live scarred and marred for the rest of my days by reason of the worst disease known to man. My looks meant much to me; they were part of my stock-in-trade, and I was proud of them. Very few survived the illness and those who did were almost always hideously scarred in the face. Oft it seemed that the greater the beauty, the worse the disfigurement. I was frantic, and this did not speed my recovery.

But youth and vitality prevailed and my fever lessened. The spots upon me turned into scabs, and they in their turn dried and fell off, leaving my face and hands mercifully clear. Even my bosom was almost entirely free from the dreaded pits, although the rest of my body was not so fortunate. I was glad of the new fashion of ruffs, for they served to conceal the scars on the sides and back of my neck. Red marks indeed there were upon my face, hands and bosom, but not pits, so I decided to stay in my room until the reddened places had died down somewhat. I missed Mary Sidney, who had nursed me with such devotion until my recovery was sure. Soon I was well enough to insist on an answer to my queries.

'Madam, my lamb,' said Kat quietly. 'Lady Mary has taken the illness.'

'Oh Jesu!' I cried. 'My fault, Kat! Does she have it badly?'

'Very badly indeed, dearest.'

'Will she live? Or has she died and I not told?'

'Nay, she will live.'

I was silent for a moment. 'Is she much disfigured?' I asked, fearfully. Kat's eyes filled with tears and I knew the answer before she nodded. 'Oh Kat,' I wept, 'how cruel is life. Is this her reward for her care of me? Where was God for her?'

'Hush, darling, hush. She has her life, remember.'

'Better be dead, say I.'

'Oh nay, she has her children and her most loving husband.'

'As to that, he is still in France and has not seen her yet. Mayhap his love will lessen when he does. Oh, it is too terrible and I feel so much to blame.'

'That is foolish,' remonstrated Kat. 'You could not help catching the pox, and to nurse you was her wish. Do not blame yourself, 'twill hinder your return to health. Rather think how you can help her, dearest, and keep her spirits up.'

'Is she well enough for me to visit her? Has the contagion gone?'

'Ay, it has, my dear, but do not be too shocked at her appearance. Keep a command over yourself, I implore you.'

So I visited Mary, who had been so very lovely, and the shock was dreadful. I can see her yet, lying there abed, her head turned on the pillow, her long black hair plaited over one shoulder. Word of God, but if I had not known it was Mary in that bed, I would not have recognised her. There was not one portion of her face that was not pitted. Her skin was like a sponge, and the once creamy complexion a sallow yellow. Her mouth was dragged down a'one side and would not close, the upper lip awry and twisted; her nose was swollen and pitted, and her beautiful large, dark eyes were large and beautiful no longer. Her eyelashes had gone, never to return, and one eye was grotesquely puffed beneath, with the upper lid swollen. The skin of the other was pulled downward to show the red within the lower lid, while the upper lid, twisted and pitted, hung low, hiding the eye itself, so that the sight of it was lost. I stood speechless and shaking, my lips trembling. From this had I escaped. My mirror told me that I would soon be as good to look upon as I had ever been. But Mary — what would she do? How to go on living so hideously disfigured? Drawing a deep breath, I stepped quietly to the bedside of my dear, poor friend.

'Mary,' I said softly, ' 'tis I, Elizabeth, come to visit you.'

At that, she started and flung herself upon her face, saying naught. I talked to her, but she would not speak to me. She pressed my hand in both her scarred ones, laying it upon her poor cheek. For sure, I could never have been so loving nor so forgiving. I sat by her bed each day until she was well enough to leave it, then I visited her in her chamber, for she would not walk abroad, and 'fore God, I could not blame her.

She and I both feared the return of Sir Henry from Le Havre, for we could not guess how he would be taken by her terribly altered looks. When he came home he was horror-struck at the sight of his wife, and who could wonder? It was desperate bad for both of them, and many said that they would part for sure, or he would take a fair mistress. But he did not, for he loved her right truly, seeming even more attentive and protective to his sad marred lady than in her days of beauty. She wore a veil over her face for the rest of her life, preferring it so. Ah, those Dudleys! They knew how to make themselves beloved, no matter how fortune failed against them.

★ ★ ★

My frettings over the French question were amply justified, for no sooner was I on my feet, tottering weakly after my dread sickness, than I received the news that Rouen had fallen, followed swiftly by the tidings that the second English garrison in Dieppe had been forced to retreat. So we held a Council meeting and decided to send reinforcements to Le Havre. Bitterly, bitterly did I grudge the good coin following bad when it was needed so greatly at home. Then the Prince of Condé, the Huguenot leader, was defeated and taken prisoner, leaving Admiral Coligny to take up command.

At home, Cecil and my councillors were ever at me to marry and secure the Succession. Since my near death of the smallpox, they had become obsessed with the matter and drove me nigh crazy with their nagging. Twenty-nine years had I now, and was no longer a girl, although I looked younger than my age and possessed great vitality of brain and body. I felt that this was because I had never been pulled down by continual child-bearing. Other ladies of my age had many children and looked far older than I, as well as being oft ailing with small torments in the belly or the back of which I knew naught. Besides, I knew well that as I was, in my virgin state, I had far better bargaining power, with myself as bait, all over Europe. None would care to offend me too seriously while they hoped to win my hand, and with it, my country.

Thanks be to Heaven, Rob had not taken the sickness from me or his sister, nor was he to be Lord Protector, which was a blessing. I made him a Privy Councillor instead, at which Cecil was not pleased, advising me to do the same for the Duke of Norfolk, my kinsman, to still any jealousy, and to balance Rob's influence. I took his advice, for as ever, it was sound.

As soon as I felt able to withstand the change, I moved myself and the Court to Windsor, for Hampton needed sweetening; we had been there long enough and 'twas beginning to stink. I had a fancy for the air of Windsor and mayhap some hunting in the Great Park, what time I was fully recovered. It was a beautiful morning, sunny and brisk like late summer, when I looked from the window to see Rob and Lord Windsor standing below with their bows and arrows, both dressed in green as if for hunting. My cousin Henry's daughter Kate was with me, I mind. Sweet Kate Carey was to become my dearest friend and companion for almost the rest of my life. So dark was she in those days, like her father, like all the Boleyns, yet in feature something like myself as was her sister Philadelphia, who was also much in my company. Pretty Ann Russell was there too, my favourite Maid-of-Honour, who was as merry as Maytime and oft made us laugh near to split. I was about to call to Rob, when an idea came to my mind, and I withdrew my head quietly. Turning to my ladies, I asked them to tell me truly if my face were indeed now unblemished. Earnestly they assured me that it was. 'Come, let us put on cloaks and hoods,' I said, 'and some of you shall go before and some behind me, so that my Lord will have to find me out. Let us go now, before they walk too far off in the park.'

So we went out and came upon Rob and Lord Windsor, with an archery butt set up in a glade, preparing to shoot a match for a wager. They looked amazed when they saw us, all giggling and wrapped as we were in our cloaks. Kate, Philadelphia and Ann went first, then I, then Katey Knollys and Frances Cobham.

'Hold, what is this?' cried Rob in exaggerated astonishment. 'Is it a band of woodland sprites come to enchant us? Where is your Queen, maidens? Is she amongst you?'

'That you must discover!' squeaked Ann in a most ridiculous disguised voice that made us laugh until we nigh fell against one another.

'Come, my Lord Windsor,' commanded Rob, 'let us put aside their hoods until we find the one we seek. For sure, she is here.'

'No need!' I laughed, throwing back my hood. 'Here I am. I had a fancy to surprise you, my Lord.' Then I told him I was recovered and never better, giving both men my hand to kiss. After that, Rob would have me hood myself and go within doors again for fear I should catch the grippe.

'Oh pooh, pooh, pooh!' I protested. 'You fuss me like some old nurse. Very well, we will leave you to your arrows and your wagering. Rob, I will see you this even. Remember it, for you are beholden to me, seeing that I have passed the pikes for your sake.'

At that, he ran to me and I signalled to my ladies to move further off, which they did, smiling knowingly, saucy wretches.

'What mean you, 'for my sake', Sweeting?' whispered Rob, his arm about me, his face close to mine.

'Why, 'twas thought of you kept me alive, I swear,' I murmured against his cheek. 'They say I spoke of you with what was near my last breath. I could not die and leave you, Rob. Heaven would be a lonely place without you.'

Sighing, he pressed me close. 'We shall be together this night,' he said, low. 'Tamworth shall guard the door. Oh my darling, thanks be to God that you are with us still.'

Gently I withdrew myself, blowing him a kiss. 'Thanks be to God and Dr. Burcot!' I called to him over my shoulder, as we left.

Dr. Burcot must have his reward, thought I. So I sent him a pair of gold spurs that had belonged to my grandsire Henry VII, and papers confirming a grant of land to him and his heirs for ever after. Land is always welcome, for a fine income may be had from it, and this should keep him in well-deserved comfort, for all England was beholden to him and his doctoring.

6

THE MATTER OF AN HEIR

December 1562 – 1564

By Yuletide, the situation in France was no better. Indeed, it seemed possible that Le Havre might be lost, and I wrote a heartening letter to Warwick to stiffen him against further assaults. In for a penny in for a pound, I thought, and trusted that Warwick would be able to hold on to Le Havre long enough to enable us to exchange it for Calais.

I heard from Tom Randolph in Scotland at this time, that a dismal Christmas had been held at the Scottish Court. I was astounded to learn that my cousin had been reduced to hysterical tears by the thunderings of the insolent preacher John Knox. Moreover, the knave had succeeded in so terrorising the Court musicians that none would sing for Mass or Evensong, and the Christmas services were all upset. Nor was there any dancing, as this was held by Knox to be of the devil. I would like to catch any saucy priest who would presume to dictate to *me* in such fashion! He would soon discover dungeon walls as powerful persuaders to obedience and a quiet tongue. There can be only one ruler in a kingdom.

In January, the second Parliament of my reign assembled, ostensibly to talk of financing the French war, but in reality to try to settle the Succession. My Commons came with a right loving petition, coupled with a fearful picture of England's condition if the Succession were to be disputed at my death. They felt that the Protestant religion was at stake, they said. They feared the Catholic faction in the land; it was full of 'contentious and malicious Papists,' as they put it.

Well, I told them fair, and did my best to soothe the admirable earnest fellows. 'Think not,' I reassured them, 'that I who in other matters have such care of you all, will be careless in this, which concerns both my own and your safety. It touches me nearer than you, my friends. You, at worst, could lose your bodies, whereas I hazard to lose both body and soul if my policy prove disastrous. I would fain defer an answer to your petition until some other time, since I will not, in so deep a matter, wade with so shallow a wit. I assure you all,' I concluded, 'that though after my death you have many stepdames, yet ye shall never have a more natural mother than I mean to be unto you all.'

So they retired, comforted but not satisfied. It would have to do; I could say no other, nor disclose my intention to use myself as a constant bait in the European marriage market, for once this intent were known, none would take me seriously as a prize. Also I wished to say nothing positive upon any subject until the finance bill was passed. After that, I meant graciously to dismiss Parliament before its members could importune me further. I was interested only in money matters at that time, for no ruler could rule without an adequate exchequer. The rest could wait.

Therefore, when a day or two later the Lords appeared at White Hall with a similar petition regarding my marriage, more delicately put, I grant, than the other, but carrying the same burden, I was irritated and annoyed. 'See you!' I cried, jumping to my feet. 'I can understand such behaviour from my Commons, where there are restless heads, in whose brains the heedless humours beat with vain judgment. But from you, my Lords, I expect less shortsighted and impetuous action than to join with the Commons, leaving me, your Queen, isolated.

If I declare a successor, gentlemen, it will cost much blood to England, and so I tell you. Look in my face,' I said. 'Look and see the marks there. They are not the wrinkles of *age*, my Lords, but the marks of smallpox! I may be twenty-nine years old,' I went on, 'and growing older every day, as you do not cease to remind me, but I am not yet in my dotage. Mayhap God will send me children as He did to Saint Elizabeth. Would that content you?'

I was growing mighty weary of their constant reference to my age and to my death as if I were some crone or ancient goodwife. I was sore afraid of old age and death, wishing to put such thoughts far behind me, and here were my members of Parliament dragging out my fears and examining them for all to see and hear. Naturally, I did not answer either petition as the suppliants had wished. It was not possible. When Parliament closed, I gave Sir Nicholas Bacon my answer to the members in a speech which I had written for him to read out. It was in a purposely involved style, and carefully so, to cover one of my *answers answerless* as they were beginning to be known.

If I had hoped to shelve the matter of an heir, I was to be rudely disappointed, for in February came news to me that I could scarce credit. Lady Catherine Grey, while yet in the Tower, had borne a second child, and another son at that, to Edward Seymour! It seemed that Sir Edward Warner, Governor of the Tower, had, in his sympathy at their pathetic plight, allowed them to spend time together, with this fertile result.

'You see how it is!' I raged to Kate Carey. 'It will be said that she should follow me, being so fruitful of sons! It could cause disaffection from the Crown, plots and factions. It is always so when the heir is known and accepted as such, especially in a position such as mine. What right had that Warner to flout my commands, how dare the fellow! He shall be dismissed! The child is a bastard at all events, since the marriage has been pronounced invalid, but he is born, and alive, for all that! Insolence! Disobedience!' I stamped up and down the chamber, flinging into the Long Gallery where all fell silent, seeing me in a fury. 'Out!' I shouted, 'get you gone, all of you. Send Cecil to me at once!'

When he came, I swung round on him so rapidly that he took an involuntary pace back from my swishing skirts. 'Another child to the Grey wench!' I stormed. 'God's death, I will not endure it, I say! They shall be parted, and thoroughly, once and for all. What could have got into Sir Edward Warner's head that he could disobey my express wish?'

'He said he did not think they would bed together, their meetings being in daylight,' answered Cecil blandly, his eyes upon the painted ceiling bosses above our heads.

'The man's a dolt!' I cried. ' 'Tis plain to me that Catherine Grey would fall pregnant at the sight of Seymour's breeches. Well, she shall have no further chance to do so. I shall send her and this latest brat to her uncle, Lord John Grey, at Pirgo in Essex, well out of the way of any more mischief. Sir Edward Warner shall cool his hot head in one of his own dungeons for a time, while he learns the meaning of obedience to his Queen.'

Cecil said naught, but his look spoke the louder. He thought me harsh to take such measure, but knew better than to say so. Well, he had not the pressures that I had, nor the ultimate responsibility for England. Those days are gone and I cannot bring them back, so it is of no use to think of what might have been. What's done is done, for good or ill.

Ill it certainly was in France, for in that same February of 1563, the Duke of Guise was shot dead and a secret treaty concluded between the Catholics and Protestants who united to force us out of France. I was

198

furious, for all had been done without a word to me or a thought for English interests. Admiral Coligny, the Huguenot leader, had taken my trust and my money and used both against me to make me look a fool. Enraged, I sent to Warwick to stay and hold Le Havre, while I sent ships of the line under the command of Admiral Clinton to harass the French sea-going craft. But in spite of the bravery of Warwick and his men, there was a creeping enemy in their midst in the shape of the plague, and 200 men died in one week. Reinforcements were rushed out, but the losses were so great that Warwick was forced to surrender Le Havre before our relief ships could enter the harbour. My Ambassador in France, Sir Tom Smith, sent urgent messages to Cecil advising him to begin peace negotiations directly. It was plain defeat, no two ways about it. Clinton's vessels were constrained to aid in the surrender and take the survivors off. Poor Warwick, jaunty to the last, his wounded leg bandaged and decorated with a large red bow to show English defiance, said sorrowfully that the plague had been more their enemy than ever were the French.

This horrid enemy he and his men brought back with them to London, and 20,000 died of it here at home. This was all we got for our

French venture — the plague and a mighty loss of funds. Some said, as some always will, that it was God's judgment. It may well have been for all I know. It certainly taught me a lasting lesson.

★ ★ ★

During the summer, Maitland of Lethington had arrived at Court to offer Scotland's help as mediator in the cursed French matter. This was not needed, the plague having done the task all too well. He also broached the subject of Marie's marriage. I smiled down at his dark, alert face as he knelt before me, for he was a personable gentleman.

'Your Majesty is in lovely looks today,' he said. It was truth, for I was not in formal dress, but attired in a most pretty loose robe of pink and silver tissue with knots on the shoulders. My hair was pushed into a silver net and my slippers were of pink silk. I had received Maitland in my small parlour, with but a few ladies and nobles in attendance. 'Thank you, William Maitland,' I said, comfortably conscious of looking my best. 'I hear your mistress wears a deal of black.'

'Ay, it is mourning for her dead husband, Madam.'

'And now you would like me to consider a live one?'

He beamed. 'Exactly so, Madam. My mistress is desirous to follow your advice to marry among the Scottish or English nobility so that the balance of power may be maintained. She wishes not to wed a man of so high a rank that her position may overshadow your own.'

I raised my brows at that. 'Indeed, I am relieved to hear it,' I said sardonically. 'I had thought that you and De Quadra were about to propose King Philip's son, Don Carlos, as a match for my cousin.' I had the satisfaction of seeing a startled look leap into his eyes. If he had imagined his conferrings with De Quadra to be secret, he was mistaken. There were no secrets at my Court but mine own.

'That would be a good match,' he stammered. 'The best she could make.'

'Yes, excellent, if she wishes to mate with a madman who is violent, so I hear. But I thought that De Quadra also felt that it would be best for her to marry a man from my hand.'

'Why,' said he, laughing uncomfortably, 'your Majesty hears all!'

'Oh, I do,' I replied. 'Make no doubt of that, Maitland. And is it not true also that you told De Quadra that I cared as little for English Protestantism as I do for the Scottish sort? Ay, and do you not regret that here, in England, we have removed the sacrament and names from our churches without reforming the abuses, as you are pleased to call them? Well, no need to protest or cavil, I know it all, so let us be plain with one another. I have a candidate for my cousin's hand.'

'Ah — ah — that is excellent,' stuttered Maitland, striving for nonchalance. 'Whom does your Majesty have in mind?'

'One who has implanted in him so many graces, that if I had a mind to wed, I would prefer him to all the world.'

'Do but tell me his name, Majesty.'

'Why,' I said affably, 'it is Lord Robert Dudley.'

There was a stunned silence. I caught Rob's eye fixed upon me in a look of horrified enquiry. Well, it was true; if I had wished to marry, I *would* have preferred him to all the world. I was well aware that he longed to wed a Queen, and that Queen would never be I. I wished him to have of the best and knew that I could trust him utterly, but to tell truth, I had put forward this proposition only to get the better of Lethington and mischievously to test Rob.

Once the words were out I could not take them back, wish them unsaid as I did, for to withdraw would have caused a diplomatic upset. So I decided to let matters run on and see what turned out. It might be a good solution after all, I thought ruefully, although I doubted Marie would take him. If she did, I would have none but myself to blame for my misery.

A few days later, Maitland came to take formal leave of me before departing for France. 'Take care,' I said, 'for I know that negotiations have begun for Queen Marie's marriage to Don Carlos and that overtures have been made to the Archduke Charles also. I tell you straight, Maitland of Lethington, that if your Queen weds either one of them I cannot avoid being her enemy. I charge her to consider well what steps she takes in such a matter. On the other hand, if she takes a person that is to my satisfaction I will not fail to be a good friend, a sister to her and make her my heir.'

And what a fuss broke about me over all this! Robert was shocked and furious at my words to Maitland. He vowed that his heart was broken, that I had treated him as a piece of furniture to be given away, that he wished none of Scotland whether as King Consort or no. He stamped and raged, he stormed and argued, pleaded and threatened, upstairs, downstairs, inside, outside, in public and in private.

'Well, yes, I know all that,' I expostulated, sticking to my guns, 'but you Rob, are the one man that I can trust in such a position. Do you not understand that? Where is your chivalry, your common-sense? Where is your pride?'

' 'Fore God, that is good!' he shouted. 'I *need* no pride when I am treated so! Where is your love for me of which you so often prate? Why, it is as if you condemn me to death. If I were such a fool as to take this Scots Queen, do you think that my head would remain on my shoulders for more than a month or two?'

'But with me behind you, you would be safe, never fear!' I cried, now exasperated more by his refusal to obey me than by feelings of love or renunciation. 'If I am ready to make a sacrifice, why should not you be?'

'All very fine!' he roared. 'Making a sacrifice is one thing; being a sacrifice is quite another. You insult me, Madam! I am not your lapdog, though you try to treat me so!'

I lost my temper, having grown used to having mine own way in all things. 'Well, I say you *are* my creature!' I yelled, loud as he. 'Without me, you are nothing, and you know it. I can never marry a subject, but I might be forced to marry out of England. I will never marry a subject, I say!'

'What do you want of me, Bess?' he said suddenly and quite quietly. 'I cannot understand you. I had thought that you would marry me, I had thought that we might be true lovers, but you deny me the completion of our love time and again. Do you want my soul as well as my body, is that it?'

I did not know the answer to that. Mayhap he was right, dear, lovely Rob. After some weeks of argument, I prevailed upon him to go, if Marie would have him. To ease his sadness, I gave him Kenilworth Castle in Warwick which had once belonged to his father, and I promised to make him Earl of Leicester at last, so that his rank would be more suitable to the proposed husband of a Queen. Indeed, I wished I had never begun the business. Rob was glum and depressed and so was I. The whole matter had grown and I knew not whether I was serious or in jest. Moreover it was unkind to Rob and I was uncomfortably aware of that all the while, which is why I lost my temper and insisted upon having my way. I wished to be a better man than any around me. I realise, now, that I was unable to give love as other women could do. It was not in me. Even if I had not been a Queen and responsible for the happiness and safety of my people and my country, I could not have given myself to any man in body or in heart. I did love Rob with all the love I was capable of giving, but it was not enough. I loved power more. There was much of the man in me, for all my femininity, and I enjoyed letting that part of me have rein. I relished having power over men, showing that a woman could do all that any man could do, and more. Sometimes I was merciless in the way I showed it, but something inside me drove me on. Most were happy enough to give in to me, and I wonder at it now, but indeed I did possess a great charm of manner and spirit, and many thus forgave me my awkward ways. Besides, there was none other able to take my place; no one had the ability of rulership as I did. It was a fact and all knew it.

★ ★ ★

We lost De Quadra that summer. The plague brought from France claimed him as a victim as well as so many others. His last year with us had been a difficult one for him, for, under the guise of his having committed an offence by allowing other persons than himself to hear Mass in his house, I had the place searched and his papers and correspondence retained. Very illuminating reading they made, with many highly personal comments upon me and my ways therein, besides valuable political information. He was also deep in debt; so much so that after his death at Durham House, his creditors refused to release his body for burial. It lay embalmed and encoffined for over a year, until his friends managed to collect enough money to have the body released and returned to his native Spain. Poor De Quadra, he was no match for me, his ways were not ours. I wished him a more rewarding time in Heaven.

Queen Marie missed him more than I, for with him went her hopes of a Spanish alliance. She sorely wished for a husband to keep her troublesome nobles in check, for she had none but her bastard half-brother Lord James Stuart, to sustain her. The strain of ruling oft made her ill, and Randolph told me that she needed marriage, being one of hot and passionate blood.

These were hard, learning years for me and England. We were forced to accept the fact that all hope of retaining Calais, or any other part of France, was at an end. It was a bitter lesson, but we are ever in God's hands and must take what He sends.

I released my Lennox cousins that year, hoping that they might have found some sense during their months of seclusion. They implored me to write to Queen Marie for the restoration of lands and titles confiscated when Lennox married his wife, and this I did in June as a gesture of goodwill, wishing bygones to be bygones. Alas for fond wishes! They came to naught. Lennox had to return to Scotland to receive his estates officially — or so Cousin Marie would have it. Right uneasy did I feel about this, delaying his leaving for as long as a year. When he went at last, a fine uproar blew up amongst my ministers, but I could detain him no longer for fear of offending Marie and causing an unpleasant incident. I insisted that he go alone, for I wished to keep the rest of his family under my eye, but I knew I had not heard the end of the affair. I cursed my good nature which had prompted me to give heed to their importunings and write that letter. It would be used against me, I was sure. So much for my Tudor relatives, thought I. They were naught but a poxy, treacherous lot when all was said and done, and bore no kindness towards me.

When Lennox left my Court, Sir James

Melville arrived there from Scotland. Some maggot entered my brain that I must prove myself better in every way than my cousin Marie. Jesu, how I paraded myself and my accomplishments before him, egged on by my admiring courtiers who would have praised my very doings on the close-stool! I laugh now in amused indulgence at my showing off, and at his struggles for diplomacy, as I pressed the poor gentleman for a definite and affirmative answer as to whether I was cleverer, taller, more musicianly, more learned, more beloved and more beautiful than his mistress of Scotland. I peacocked before him, clad in costume after costume, my hair dressed a score of different ways, all mighty fetching. I confused his ears with a very Babel of foreign tongues; I played the lute, the clavichord, the cittern, each tune more complicated than the last, and ever and anon, I asked: 'Does your mistress wear this, speak this, play this, do this, as well as I?'

My old head wags in deprecation of such behaviour, most undignified and unQueenly, but I cared not a rap for that then. For all my show, I think he preferred his Scottish Queen to me. In spite of all his careful and complimentary answers, I could not make him change his mind, and this drove me on. He must have thought me a prideful, forward virago, and he was right, I fear. Yet he liked me I could tell, and I found him very easy company. I mind that I took him to my bedchamber one evening, and while he held the candle, I opened my little cabinet wherein I kept divers small pictures wrapped in paper with the names writ in my own hand on the paper. Upon the first I drew out was writ *My Lord's Picture*. Melville begged for a sight of it, so I unwrapped it and showed him a miniature of Rob.

'I keep him close to me at all times,' I said. 'In body by day and in miniature, here, by night.' He smiled knowingly, remarking that the miniature was indeed fortunate. Wrapping up the portrait to replace it in the cabinet, I gave him a gleaming look and laughed, but enlightened him no further.

Rob and I were both thirty-one years old that year and at the height of our beauty. This was the year that I created him Earl at last. Eh, how I remember that day. I need not even close my eyes to recall it, for it assembles before me like a moving, talking picture. I see myself there at St. James's, all in white, my hair in fiery curls topped by a jewelled coronet. My eyes are bright, my red lips smile, I am as straight and slender as any young willow tree. There, arranged about the Presence Chamber, is the entire

Court, a rainbow of colours, a galaxy of jewels, a hothouse of perfume and sweat. Melville is there and the dark, fascinating, new Spanish Ambassador Don Guzman de Silva. The peers stand stately in their crimson robes, the heralds nearby, gilded trumpets ready to blow the blast of triumph.

At my feet kneels my darling, his proud head bent, his face grave and solemn, at which ponderous look I am forced to smile, but so lovingly! And whose is this visage that swims before me out of the crowd? It is that of young Henry Darnley, elder son of my cousin of Lennox, a tall, baby-faced, pretty-looking youth, who holds the Sword of State by virtue of his position as first Prince of the Blood Royal. There are some who would wish to see him as Marie's husband. I hear the impressive words of dedication read from the parchment with its seals and ribbons, and I take up the ceremonial mantle of ermine and miniver with my own hands and lay it over the shoulders of my love. Now my wrinkled face smiles and my old eyes close as I recall what I did next . . .

'*The Queen sleeps*,' my ladies whisper, by the fire at Richmond. '*Hush, let us not disturb her, she is old and tired and needs her rest.*'

Your Queen does not sleep, ladies, for all

211

that her eyes are shut. She but lives a most favoured part of her past . . .

Well, I could not resist it. I had to touch him, ceremony or no. As I settled the mantle about his broad shoulders, I allowed my fingers to slide into the collar and caress his strong, brown neck. At once his eyes flew up to meet mine and he flushed a deep crimson, beloved knave. I held his gaze for a moment, then allowed mine to rove about the chamber. As I suspected, shocked faces, reproving faces, amused faces too — but these were fewer. My mild look changed to one of frowning hauteur, and I had the satisfaction of seeing all countenances straighten themselves to a plate-like nullity as the trumpets rang out and the new Earl of Leicester rose to his feet, his hand in mine, to be presented to the Court.

'And how do you like our new Earl?' said I to Melville, waiting with cynical amusement for his smooth reply.

'Why, Majesty, he is a worthy servant, fortunate in his Princess who is so well able to discern and reward good service,' he answered suavely.

I nodded. 'Aye. Yet you like better yon long lad,' I countered, swinging about to point my finger at young Darnley nearby. Melville looked slightly startled and I laughed. 'Oh yes, Sir James, I know of certain Scottish hopes in that quarter. Did you think I did not?'

He shook his head at once. 'Why, Madam, no lady of spirit would make choice of such a man who resembles a woman more than a man. I think no one would wish that,' he lied.

'Certainly I would not make such a choice,' I replied. 'But might not the Queen of Scotland?'

'I cannot say,' he answered hastily, 'but I trust not. Lord Darnley is but a foolish boy.'

7

DESTINY WITH MEN FOR PIECES PLAYS

Spring 1565 to December 1566

As I had guessed, it was not long before Matthew Lennox sent, asking me to allow his son, Lord Darnley, to join him in Scotland. It had been neatly done, I had to give my cousin credit for that. Marie had kept my letter supporting Lennox's request for the restoration of his estates by her, there it was in black and white in my own hand. There was little I could do, although at first I refused to let the lad go. Sentiment apart, Rob would have been of inestimable use to me as Marie's husband, but she was now using the Succession question as a bargaining point, letting me know that she would not accept Rob unless I made her my official heir, and this I was in no hurry to do. As well as this, Rob and Cecil both thought I should let Darnley go and hope for the best. At least Darnley would be better than a foreign Catholic if it ever came to that.

Well, marriage is a fateful risk, be it

planned never so carefully. There were many weddings in the next twelve-month, weddings and a death. I feel the tears rise behind my eyes as I lie here wrapped in furs in my cold, old age, remembering that death. Oh Kat, my best, my dearest, I miss you still and will do until I follow you to the grave and beyond.

So I will think of the weddings instead. There was Ann Russell's marriage to Ambrose Dudley. That was a gay affair, and my little Ann became Countess of Warwick. I was pleased with the match and so was her father, the Earl of Bedford. We held the ceremony at White Hall in the Chapel Royal and the breakfast was eaten, very merry, in the Council Chamber. It was at this wedding that we all wore the new starch in our ruffs. Such excitement as it caused then; seen by the stern and moralising-minded as the Devil's liquor. Well, I cared not for the Devil, even if starch were his liquor; I found it most exact for my ruffs, holding them up and out as never before. The stuff came from Holland, brought by a Mevrouw Dinghen who undertook to stiffen ruffs for ten angels apiece, which I thought excessive. I had my own starch-maid, Mistress Boonen, to stiffen my ruffs or picardils for me. There was a tailor called Higgens, I mind me, who had a shop in a lane near St. James's. He would stitch gold and silver broidery over the picardils. His custom was great and his shop always full, so I heard, and he wrought some for me, very fine, all covered with little moons and stars in silver thread. In time, the lane itself was called The Picardilla, and is so still, after Master Higgens and his picardil-work.

Another wedding was that of the daughter of my cousin Katey Knollys to Walter Devereux, Viscount Hereford. This girl was called Lettice and was second-cousin to me, very pretty, with the red Tudor hair, the dark Boleyn eyes and the delicate, regular Knollys features. Methought she had a great conceit of herself for one so young, and sure, she was monstrous petted and indulged; too quick and pert altogether for my taste, although at first I felt a certain warmth towards her for my dear Katey's sake. I was to find that I had not heard the last of smart young cousin Lettice, married off early though she might be. Such airs she gave herself as Lady Hereford and later as Countess of Essex, prinking and pranking about, gaudy as a dragon-fly and as noticeable. She was jealous of me, that Lettice; pushful, vain and haughty, and what a blow was she to strike me! Eh dear, I wished her dead many a time, the saucy strumpet, for the sly, wounding, heart-breaking trick she later played on me. I slapped her face for it and struck as hard as I could. I wish I could have killed her, kin though she was to me, the bitch. I will not have her near me and I care not where she ends her heartless days. She is alone now and a widow once more after the death of her third husband, Sir Christopher Blount, and he young enough to be her son, shame on her!

Why, she took my darling from me in years to come, married him all secret and nary a word to me who loved him so dear. Ay, she was a real Honey-Hot-a-Bed, that one. No sooner was my Rob, my heart's love, in his grave, than she was to the altar with young Sir Kit. Well, she made but little of it in the end, in money or happiness. I have no pity for her, the false cat, may she rot in hell, for that is where she will go, for sure, when her time comes.

Think of weddings will I? There were two more in that year of 1565, and neither with my pleasure or approval. They happened after June time and one of the saddest months of my life. Kat, Kat, how could you slip away so, and me not at your side? Oh, but I was as broken-hearted as the wretchedest, poorest, most simple maid

217

in the land. Darling one, she had seemed more tired than usual, a little short of breath, but after all she was fifty-one. Most of us age fast in our fifties, growing wrinkled and grey. I never guessed that she was like to die. Why, I thought — if I thought at all — that she would go on for ever.

She was abed at my last sight of her. I felt somewhat concerned, for it was not like her to lie up. 'How now, Kitty-Kat!' I said to her rallyingly. 'What is it with you? Are you turned slug-a-bed?'

She smiled up at me. 'Nay, my darling, only tired. If I do aught, my heart pounds in my breast fit to burst and my head grows somewhat dizzy. It is nothing for you to fret your pretty head over. You have enough of cares, my Queen.'

I drew up a stool to the side of the bed. She did look pale, with a greyish tinge round the mouth and a blue look to her lips. 'Kat,' I said slowly, 'are you sure you are only tired? You are not ill, are you? What a thoughtless creature I am, with my mind full of my own affairs! You would tell me if you felt truly unwell, would you not?'

'Of course I would, love. 'Tis naught. I am growing old, thou knowest, and am not so spry as I was. It comes to us all sooner or later. We cannot escape old age unless we die young.'

'Ay, but Kat, I am not used to seeing you tired. See, I will sit with you and we shall have some wine and laugh together, shall we?'

I stayed with her for the rest of the day, and we talked much of old times. She told me how proud she was of me, how she loved me, and how I had brought all of happiness to her. She spoke of Rob, and how she had feared I would bring myself trouble through him.

'Nowadays I do not worry about that,' she said, 'for I see that you can deal with any eventuality that life lays before you. You are a great woman, darling heart, a great Queen, and will be greater yet.'

I kissed her fondly. 'Ah, I am your ewe lamb, am I not? Now, it grows late, Kat beloved, and you and I must rest. Sleep you well, and I will come to you tomorrow.'

'Ay, do that, my love. Good night and God bless you.'

We kissed again and I left her. Those were her last words to me, for she died early the next morning. The shock and the grief nigh turned my brain. I was as one changed into stone for several days; unable to weep, unable to eat, unable to sleep. My Kat was gone for ever. She had left me at last, the support of my life. No one could take her place, be they ever so fond, ever so loving. I was bereft. I felt that half myself had gone with her, my Kat, my dearest, my heart of hearts. When the tears came, I wept for hours, night and day, on and on, my eyes like rivers, my throat a raw storm of sobs that rent and choked me. I went from one migraine to another, calling upon her who had gone, calling her to return to her Bess who loved her so dear. But she had left me for ever and I would see her sweet face no more on this earth. It was agony, and my heart throbs with it still, near forty years later. There was no one like you, my best, my more-than-mother. God grant that we meet in Heaven, for part of my youth went with you who taught me how to laugh and how to live. May God and His angels bless you and keep you in peace and joy until we meet again.

★ ★ ★

Before I had time to recover from my grief, Queen Marie of Scotland married Lord Darnley of Lennox. Here was a feather in the cap of my cousin Margaret. Cousin to one Queen, now mother-in-law to another, she saw herself as a personage of great consequence and gave herself a thousand unpleasant airs to match, the nasty creature. I sent her and her airs to the Tower for her pains.

In the end, I had allowed Henry Darnley to join his father in Scotland. Well served indeed was I for my lenience and a fine fool had I been made to look in the eyes of the world. I had blinked mine own but once too often in the direction of Scotland, that was for sure. I knew that Darnley was looked upon with favour by the Catholics, both in England and Scotland, but I did not dream that my cousin would ever fancy him. For my part, there was nothing in him to fancy, long and thin as a drink of water, with a soft, pretty lady's face at the top. He was yellow-haired too, and I ever favoured dark men. But she fell crazy-mad in love with the lad, surrounded as she was with old and ugly Scots, and having been wed before to a sick, mother's darling of a child. She had no experience of a proper man to measure him by, and would have him or none.

I could not relax my vigilance of Scotland for a moment after that. When I think that she could have had my Rob! Well, her loss was my gain, although he could have been my right hand as her King-consort. That Darnley fool did not love my cousin, only her

rank and what would come to him through
her. He was of no more use to her than a
pain in the backside, although his catamites
suffered that, for he preferred little boys as
it turned out, although a woman would do
if no boy were to be had. A drunken sot he
was too, constantly in his cups, bragging and
swaggering about the Scottish Court, until
none minded him nor respected him. Still,
he did have enough manhood to get Marie
pregnant, although I was sorry for the babe
to be sired by such a father.

Cecil prophesied that no good would come
of the match. 'Carnal marriages begin with
happiness and end in strife,' he said gravely
to me. I feared most greatly that he would
prove to be right.

If this were not enough, the next month
brought another shock, this time from the
youngest lady of the Grey family, the stunted
and pug-faced Lady Mary. At the age of
twenty-five I would have given her credit
for more sense, but she was a true daughter
of that brood. When I think of the slyness,
the deceit of her, sneaking out through the
Privy Chamber to the Council Room to
send a message to her intended bridegroom,
and he none but Tom Keyes, my serjeant-
porter! She, a Maid-of-Honour, a lady in
succession to the throne of England, to

behave so! No person of her rank and standing could wed without the Sovereign's permission, but to so demean herself with a serjeant-porter! It passed all belief. They were married in Keyes' room at the Water-gate of Westminster Palace, by an unknown priest, of course. If I had caught the fellow, I would have had him unfrocked, by the stars I would. Oh, I near had an apoplexy over the business. Such a laughing stock she made of herself too, with him well over six feet high and she but four feet tall in her high-blocked pattens. All were a-snort and a-snicker over the affair.

So off went he to the Fleet Prison, and she to Chequers in Buckinghamshire in the custody of William Hawtrey. I kept her there for a while, then moved her to Placentia, under the eye of Kate Willoughby of Suffolk, her grandfather's widow and last wife. I did not allow the pair to live together. I could not have a serjeant-porter's brat as a possible claimant to the throne. After three years I released Keyes on the understanding that he lived in seclusion at Lewisham and stayed away from his foolish wife. Jane was the only one of that family with any scrap of sense, and much good it did her, poor child. As for the rest, they were better lechers than learners.

At Windsor that summer, I was cross and cantankerous and could not be still. I would dance, walk, hunt, ride, until my ladies were wearied almost to death. I quarrelled with Rob and snapped at everyone else, for my nerves were all a-twangle, fretting so sorely as I was for Kat. I took up with young Tom Heneage to please myself and to provoke Rob. Indeed, I acted the part of a cold, fickle-hearted jade full well. Some demon entered into me so that I played one man against the other for the sheer excitement of it. It was unkind and thoughtless, but it seemed to make up, somehow, for the lack in myself. It helped to cover the misery of the loss of Kat just a little and could lead to naught, I reasoned, since Tom was already wed. Rob was provoked indeed, but not in the way that I had intended. Nay, he showed his teeth, did my love, he was no ladies' lap-dog. He chose to play me at my own game, and the playmate he chose was Lettice Knollys, to my chagrin. Then he asked for leave of absence to stay at his own house, as other men were allowed to do, a thing he had never asked before, being happy to remain always at my side. I gave him no answer at first, being too upset, but in a few days I sent for him. My oath, but we had a quarrel, and before the whole Court.

He roared that I had cast him aside and had no heart, treating him as a plaything and no man, while I shouted that he was not my ruler. Let him imagine no such thing, I screeched, for here there was but one mistress and no master! We screamed and yelled ourselves hoarse, until I, feeling tears near, rushed to seek the privacy of my chamber. Of course, we were reconciled, but I had hurt and humiliated Rob more than I knew, and had made him aware of Lettice, fool that I was.

★ ★ ★

I was still being sought in marriage by the Archduke Charles, except that now he was a little less impulsive in declaring his eagerness for the match. His brother, Maximilian II, the new Holy Roman Emperor, had sent his personal envoy to England to discover my intentions. Apparently the Archduke had no desire to be led by the nose a second time. My intentions were quite decided, but I did not inform the Archduke or his brother's envoy of them. I intended to keep all on a string and be caught by none, and so said different things to each, ensuring that the issue was well clouded and all remained eager to please England and me. Cecil favoured the

Archduke's suit, as I guessed he would, for he had a dislike to Rob as an upstart and a place-seeker. I smiled on all and went my own way, telling none what was in my mind.

So matters went on, with tempers running high at Court as Rob and my cousin Norfolk, always at outs, began a jealous feud, which I finally settled by choosing both men to be invested as Knights of the Order of St. Michel by the French King. This Order should, by right of Sovereignty, have come to me, but I, being a woman, was considered ineligible to receive it, which I thought utter twaddling nonsense. However, I overcame my annoyance and put the situation to good use by allowing the two hot-heads to share the award and so grow a little cooler.

In Scotland, affairs were most unstable. Queen Marie's adviser, her Protestant, bastard half-brother, the Lord James Stuart, Earl of Moray, had left the Scottish Court through dislike of Henry Darnley. When requested to appear before his Queen, he refused to do so, declining to explain his behaviour, and with good reason, for he had decided to raise a rebellion and needed England's support for it. After a very rapid skirmish called the Chaseabout Raid, Marie emerged victorious and outlawed him. Mayhap she had heard of his constant appeals to me for aid and money and thought him better out of the way.

During September, in order to soothe alarmed Protestants, I did give him a half-hearted promise of asylum in England if he should need it, and within a month he had fled over the Border into England. Protestants or no, I did not want Lord James; still less now that his sister had proved the victor in their struggle. If I were seen openly to champion Lord James, this could cause a war with Scotland. Rather than that, he and his Protestants could go whistle down the wind, and I would have to tell him so. I sent my messengers to halt him at Royston and bring him in secret to me at dusk of the next evening, when I explained my position to him, at the same time refusing support for his rebellion.

'I cannot do it, Lord Moray,' I said flatly. 'You must see that for me to do so would be to plunge us into war, and this I will not have for all the gold of Spain or jewels of the Indies.' He mumbled something about 'religion' and 'right'. I was swift to interrupt him. 'Right, you say? Your sister has the right, my lord, and naught can be done about that. As for religion, there is time to see how matters run. Now hear me. It is necessary for us to conceal any attitude of friendship between us. I have not said that I am your friend, nor will I. In fact, the world must know that I am against you and your rebel companions. I must say it in public, you understand? Sovereign may not stand against Sovereign unless the reason be overwhelming, and even then should be viewed with caution. Also. De Foix, the French Ambassador, is to visit me in order that France may see how severely I deal with rebels, and in this you must play your part. I shall have to reprimand you most forcefully before him, and you must take it like a man and a penitent.'

This he promised to do and acquitted himself well next day, showing a chagrin that was not all assumed. After the French Ambassador had taken himself off, I spoke again to Lord Moray, saying that if he raised no riots in my country I would try to intercede with Marie for him, as far as I could. He had chosen to reside in Newcastle, so I charged him to live there quiet and peaceably.

When he had left my presence, I called Cecil to me. 'Keep friendly with him,' I murmured. 'It might be advisable. I cannot show him more than good manners, but you can, Cecil. See to it.'

What in other men might have been classed as a grin passed over his face, hastily concealed by his hand. His bright, grey eyes twinkled into mine. 'My mind exactly, Madam,' he said. 'The right hand knows not what the left doeth. As a token of respect, a goodly horse well-caparisoned, and some few funds in a bag await Lord James' departure.'

'Oho, Sir Spirit! Think you to beat me at my own game?'

He chuckled. 'I? Never, Majesty. I strive but to keep up with you.'

'Well, well,' I smiled, ' 'tis always best to swing with the prevailing wind so long as it blows to our advantage. Keep me informed of Lord James' movements.'

In March of 1566 came the news from Scotland of the murder of Queen Marie's secretary before her eyes and in her presence. The man Rizzio had been much favoured by her, some saying that he was the father of her coming child, but I discounted this as so much nasty talk. I found the report of his murder and her treatment almost unbelievable. She was pushed and threatened with a dagger by the consumptive Lord Ruthven, and held against the wall by her drunken husband, while the bleeding, screaming Rizzio was dragged forth and finished off outside on the stairs. I shook my head in amazement at such tidings. What kind of control had she over her Court that her nobles should treat her, their Queen, in such fashion? Sure, it would never happen in England! To add to the beastliness of the business, her husband, Henry Darnley, had been among the plotters, swearing loudly that the child was Rizzio's and none of his, and that he should be made King in her stead, she being unfitted to rule.

'Christ, she is six months gone with child,' I said to Rob's younger sister, Kitty Dudley, now Lady Huntingdon. 'She might well miscarry of the babe.'

'Indeed she might, Madam. It is expected, she being a weakly lady.'

But she did not. In spite of all, she held the child, bringing forth a son on the 19th of June, after a cruel labour. Ah, I mind well the day on which the news was brought to me. We were at Placentia. The weather was golden and all was merry as we danced in the evening of the 23rd of June. I was showing the steps of a new dance to an applauding crowd, when Cecil appeared at my side and whispered in my ear.

'The Scottish Queen is lighter of a fair son, Madam,' he breathed. 'He is but four days old.'

I felt the blood drain from my face, for I experienced an almost bodily shock at these words. The news was not unexpected but it struck upon me like a blow. I even staggered a step before I found my chair, lowering myself into it stiffly like an old woman. Glancing around at the surprised and concerned faces about me, I said in a difficult voice: 'The Scottish Queen is lighter of a fair son.' I drew a deep breath, but could not be composed. 'And I am but a barren stock!' I blurted out in half-choked tones, before I could check myself.

Soon after, I went to my room, there to pace up and down, weeping and agonised. Never, never would I be the mother of a fair son, or any child. My throne would not go to the bone of my bone. I ached, I longed, I was rent with the pangs of denied motherhood. And I denied my own self. It was like a huge mountain that I could not climb, a mighty door that resisted all my batterings, for my fear was greater than desire, implanted there since my baby days when I had learned that marriage meant death.

When the next morning came, I was able to show a brave face to Sir James Melville, greeting him with a laugh and a few steps of La Volta, the new dance. I sent my heartiest wishes to Marie and agreed to stand godmother to the babe, who was to be called James. I chose the Countess of Argyll as my proxy and sent the Earl of Bedford to Scotland as my representative, bidding him take in his baggage a golden font worth £1,000 for the christening. 'It will do also for the next child borne by our good sister,' I said as gaily as I could.

* * *

That autumn I had a great tussle with my Parliament which I had been forced to summon through lack of funds. I was reluctant to do so, for I knew that the Succession question would be aired again, especially since the birth of Prince James. Indeed, folk seemed to speak and think of little else. For the first time since the reign of my sister, impertinent broadsheets were printed and left in the streets and churches, even in my own chamber. I was furious, for they all took me to task over my tardiness in providing an heir for England. Merchants talked it over in their counting-houses, students at Lincoln's Inn debated it, the wretched business hummed in the very air. All were deadly feared over the fact that it was my life alone that stood between a Scottish monarch upon the throne in the person of little Prince James, or disputes involving the right of Catherine Grey or Margaret Strange to inherit, leading the country to the edge of civil war. But, holding to my policy, I was determined to name no one, no matter how pressed thereto, and I would have to face this most unwelcome matter whether I liked it or no.

I cursed the lack of money that had so constrained me to call Parliament, but it had to be, there was no other way. The Treasury was so low after the disaster of the French war that more funds were needed, and only Parliament could give consent to this. It was soon apparent that consent would not be given unless I made a decision about my marriage. One hardy fellow had jumped to his feet during a meeting of the Commons.

'I recall that the Queen received funds in the last Parliament three years ago!' he had shouted. 'She promised then to wed or declare a Succession. Now the funds are gone and she is still unmarried. No answer, no money!'

I was enraged when told of it. No matter how Cecil tried to keep them to the business of accounting for the war expenses, the saucy fellows would have none of it. I was much angered and spoke roundly to them all. 'My Commons are very rebellious,' I said, loud and sharp. 'It is not for you to stay my affairs and it does not become a subject to compel a Sovereign. You little realise what you demand in this,' I went on. 'It is to dig my grave before I am dead. You would never have dared such presumption in my father's time, by God! I am a Prince!' I shouted, 'and I say again that it is not fit for subjects to meddle in the affairs of a Prince! Marriage is my own business and I will keep it so. I tell you, that if I need protection from my own Parliament — and it seems that I do — I will marry indeed, and someone that you neither like nor desire! I would remind you that all the laws which you make, sirs, are nothing without my consent and authority. I shall take counsel with those who understand law and justice, for the whole matter is too important to be declared to a knot of hare-brains!'

I would move no further, argue and rant as they would. They did not understand my feelings. How could they, when all was said and done? I withdrew into silence and privacy like a cornered beast. I would not, could not do as they wished. It was an impossibility beyond sense or reason. I spent the next few days struggling to conceal my fear and despair behind a stony face and stony silence. The House of Lords, led by Cousin Norfolk, joined forces with the Commons against me to fight this battle of wills. Norfolk was heard to say that I was to blame for refusing to take any other advice than mine own. I was furious and broke my silence, shouting that he was an impertinent traitor who deserved imprisonment for such words.

After almost a week, I received my ministers again. There they stood before me; Rob, Will Parr of Northampton, my bluff uncle Lord William Howard, and Will Herbert of Pembroke. 'See you,' I said hopefully, speaking them fair. 'Tom Norfolk was wrong to speak so in public. I am sure you agree, my Lords.'

'Nay, Madam,' answered Will Herbert, 'it is not right to treat the Duke of Norfolk badly, since he and the others were but doing what they thought right for the good of the country. It was their duty to speak.'

'Ay,' I flashed, 'and to speak is all you can do, Pembroke. Loud and windy, like some swaggering soldier. We all know you love the sound of your own words!'

Having silenced Pembroke, I rounded on Will Parr, brother to my father's last wife. 'And you, my Lord Marquis,' I exclaimed, 'what do you here? You, with your tangled marriages, you are of no account in this affair. Do not try to mince words with me sir,' I barked, as he made to speak. 'Rather than talk about *my* marriage, you had better talk about the arguments used to help you to wed again with a wife still living! What about that, my Lord?'

Agitated and upset, I turned to Rob. 'You, my Lord, you!' I cried. 'If all the world abandoned me, I thought that you would be true!'

Down on his knees fell Rob. 'Madam, my dearest, how can you say this. You know I am wholly devoted to you, ready to die at your feet!'

'Oh, get up do!' I snapped, near to tears. 'Dying at my feet has nothing to do with the matter! You are against me with these others. How dare you all defy me so!' I stormed. 'My Lords Leicester and Pembroke, you are banned from the Presence Chamber for furthering the Succession question in Parliament without my allowance. I will not have it!' I cried, my voice breaking with distress. 'Now, get you gone, all of you!'

A se'ennight or so later, I heard that a petition was to come to me from Parliament. In order to forestall this, I ordered thirty members from each house to come before me so that I could explain my position to them. When they appeared, I spoke to them

236

long and vehemently, telling them as best I could of my deep feelings, promising that I would deal in the Succession for their safety and without their interference.

'It is monstrous,' I finished severely, 'that the feet should direct the head. Now you may go, good sirs, and I promise that you shall have the benefit of my prayers.'

They were not satisfied, of course, although by this time much hot blood had cooled. In the end, I resolved the deadlock by asking for only two-thirds of the monies I had previously requested. Parliament agreed to this, and a Subsidy Bill was drawn up for me to sign. Imagine my annoyance when I read in it of my promise to wed! As this Bill would be made public, I ordered the offending sentences to be stricken out, refusing to sign until this was done, scribbling a message to the effect at the bottom of the paper.

At last it was re-written to my liking, saying that: ' . . . *the Queen had graciously allowed she would marry at her convenience.*' It was ambiguous enough and Parliament would have to be content with it. I had won a notable victory.

8

In Scotland, matters went from bad to worse.
Marie had refused to live with the weak and
vicious Henry Darnley and was staying at the
Earl of Mar's estate at Alloa with her child.
She wished to divorce her husband, but was
advised not to attempt this, as doubts over
the paternity of Prince James had already
been circulated. As for Darnley, few wished
for the company of one who had publicly
betrayed his fellow conspirators — thus a
traitor twice over. He did not appear at
his son's christening in December, I heard,
being afraid to show his face to humiliation
and contempt, and no wonder. I suspected
that he was jealous of the attention paid to
Marie and the babe; it would have been
typical of him and his brood. Afterwards, he
returned to the Lennox lands near Glasgow,
announcing that he meant to fly to Flanders
and publish his grievances to the world.

'By Heaven,' said I to Cecil, 'if he does

that, the world will be convinced for sure that the Prince is not truly his own.'

'Well, Madam,' answered Cecil, 'Queen Marie called a Council meeting to deal with this. Lord Darnley had returned to Edinburgh, but refused to enter even the gates of Holyrood Palace while the Lords of the Council were within.'

'Scarcely surprising,' I replied drily. 'I daresay he fears to be a second Rizzio at their hands and not without reason.'

Cecil nodded. 'The Queen, realising this,' he continued, 'dismissed the Council and guards and came out to greet Lord Darnley herself, persuading him to enter and reassuring him that his fears were unfounded. She took him to her own rooms and there he stayed all night.'

'H'm,' quoth I, 'she is a good actress, methinks, and he is easily gulled, poor fool.'

So we waited for more news. It was evident that Darnley was hopelessly outclassed in wits and brain by all those about him, including his wife, who obviously could lead him by the nose if she so wished. I could see no comfortable resolution for him who was not quick-thinking nor close-mouthed, as was amply proved when he was forced to attend a Council meeting at which Du

Croc, the French Ambassador to Scotland, was present in order to send a report for France.

Darnley was asked if he intended to leave Scotland for France, and if so, why so. He knew not what to say and the Councillors told him that if he acted in this manner, abandoning the society of her to whom he was so far obliged, the whole world would blame him as an ingrate. 'And then,' went on Cecil, recounting the news, 'the Queen spoke affectionately to him, beseeching him that he would at least be pleased to declare, before the Lords, whereby she had offended him in anything. She took his hand lovingly and implored him for God's sake to declare if she had given him any occasion for his resolution to leave, at which he stood mumchance, stammering and mumbling, biting his lips. Then one of the Councillors asked him how he could leave so beautiful a Queen and so noble a realm.'

'Well, did he not say that his wife seemed to dislike him, that he had no authority, that the Lords scouted him and treated him with contempt?' I asked impatiently.

'Nay, for he would have had to speak of Rizzio's death and his double-dealing in that.'

'Dear God, such a fool should never aspire

to villainy! What next?' I looked hard at Cecil. It seemed that he had not told me all. 'Is there more? Is there something that you are keeping from me?'

' 'Tis but rumour, Madam, and I do prefer factual information. We know but too well that Lady Rumour can lie, and much trouble may be caused by hearkening to her words.'

'A fig for your preaching! Tell me. I will keep my own counsel.'

So he told me that after her son's birth and after Darnley had retired to Glasgow, it was thought that Marie had taken the Earl of Bothwell as her lover, even though he had been recently wed to Lady Jean Gordon. 'In fact,' declared Cecil, with a glimmering smile, 'he has refused all our bribes, Madam.'

Our eyes met and I gave a laugh. 'Oh. Well, he does have a weakness along another direction, does he not?'

'Yea, Madam. He is an almighty lecher, and in this rumour does not lie. He is a good soldier, too. Seemingly the Queen found the combination irresistible and showed her feelings plainly.'

I laughed again. 'She shocked the strait-laced Scots by that, I'll wager. I know how my ministers glare on my fondness for

241

Rob,' I said, wrinkling my nose roguishly at Cecil.

He shook his head at me, smiling. 'Your Majesty will have your jest. But whatever you and Lord Leicester do, you keep it within bounds — or attempt to do so at anyrate.'

'Puritan!' I cried, my eyes twinkling. 'Leave me alone, I need no censure from you! What else of Marie and Lord Bothwell?'

'Lord Bedford tells me that he carries all credit in the Scots Court and is much hated as a result. Some say he is a second Rizzio.'

'Nonsense. Rizzio was never her lover.'

'Very true. But neither did Rizzio rape her.'

'What!' I cried. 'You mean that Bothwell raped her? My God, how so? Did she not punish him, call the Lords, tell her brother Lord Moray? Why was not Bothwell imprisoned for such *lèse-majesté?*'

'It seems that she was at the Checker House in the Cow Gate at Edinburgh, supervising the accounts, he and several courtiers with her. Soon they were left alone and it was then that the mischief happened.'

'But why did she not complain or raise the alarm?'

'It caused her to fall deep in love with him, Madam. She is utterly besotted, I hear, and will not allow him to leave her side or her bed, so goes the story. She is mad for him, they say.'

'But might she not become pregnant, Cecil?'

' 'Tis said that she is already two or three months gone, Madam.'

I was speechless. I saw no way out of this coil if Marie refused to be reconciled to her husband, and this she was obviously now set against. It was plain to me that she was one who would put desire before duty any day; her people, her realm, could go hang, but she must have her way. It was true that her womanhood had had no real flowering, that she had never experienced the delights of the flesh and that she was a hot-blooded, passionate woman. I understood that. But she was also a Queen and a ruler. To be a woman and a reigning Queen is no easy thing; to accomplish the fruition of both, one must make sacrifices and compromises. If not, the womanhood is like to be lost and the throne as well. She never learned it, nor ever would. I turned to Cecil. 'How the devil will she resolve this, think you? What can she do?'

'She is ill and has taken to her bed,' he said. 'Mayhap to collect her thoughts and decide upon her future actions.'

'It would be fortunate should Darnley die of the smallpox from which he suffers! It would be a way out of her plight. Nay, I am wrong there, for if she is breeding and all know that Darnley could not have been the father, how is she to account for her state? She cannot marry Bothwell, for he is wed already.'

Cecil raised his brows. 'Divorce?' he suggested dubiously.

'But she is ardent Catholic!' I protested. 'There will have to be an almighty forswearing to accomplish that end. Besides, she will lose the respect of all if she gives countenance to divorce.'

'We shall have to wait and see,' replied Cecil, shrugging resignedly. 'I fear it will cause a great upset whatever she does.'

And a great upset was caused, by God! More like an earthquake or a thunderbolt it was when it happened on the 10th of February in 1567. The news was brought to me and rushed off to all the Courts of Europe, likewise, that King Darnley was dead indeed. Not of the smallpox, that was sure. Nay, to be blown up with gunpowder, strangled, and left naked in a snow-covered field was his dreadful fate. I was horror-stricken, and when Sir Robert Melville, brother to Sir James, gave me the awful tidings, I gasped, with my hand to my heart, scarce believing my ears as he told me that Darnley was thought to have been murdered, and that Marie herself was suspected to have had a hand in it. I shook my head, refusing at first to believe such a thing, saying that it was too terrible to contemplate. But I had to discover more, so that I could perhaps sift the truth for myself, so I plied Sir Robert with agitated questions, finding that Lord Darnley had been staying in a house in a lonely spot just outside Edinburgh when he met his death.

'For you see, Madam,' explained Sir Robert, scarce knowing where to look, 'Queen Marie had persuaded him to her side again, and because his attack of pox was still like to infect others, she decided that this house in Kirk o' Field would be better for him to dwell in than Edinburgh Castle, where he might pass on the contagion. Then she recollected that she had promised to attend some wedding festivities, and so left him at eleven o'clock that night.'

'So she was absent when the explosion took place?'

'Indeed so, your Grace.'

'Now all will be mourning,' I said reflectively. 'We must show respect here, too. I will order Court mourning for him.' As I spoke, I noticed that Sir Robert was looking

245

uncomfortable, as if I had embarrassed him. 'What is it, man?' I cried. 'Out with it. I will know!'

He said that the royal widow had retired to her chamber for one day only, and that was the extent of the official mourning for her husband. No further instructions had been given. I stared round at those surrounding me as I sat upon my chair of state, for Sir Robert's visit was a formal one. My astonishment at such casual behaviour was mirrored on every face.

'She must be prostrated with grief and away from her mind with shock, poor creature,' I said, seizing upon the most charitable explanation of such conduct as occurred to me at the moment. 'I must write to her at once; there must be something I can do to help her.'

So I began a letter to her and the words came straight from my heart. While I was at the business, I recollected Darnley's mother, my cousin Margaret Lennox. She was still in the Tower, but enjoying every comfort there. She would need comfort now, indeed, to withstand this fearful blow. I chose Cecil's sweet wife and kind Lady Howard to break the dread news to her rather than go myself, for she had never liked me, and would take it far worse from my lips, thinking me to have

246

had aught to do with it, or some such. As it was, she became so disturbed in her mind with grief that I had to send my own doctor to her, and soon afterwards sent her back to Sheen with Sir Richard Sackville, where she saw Robert Melville and heard his account of the affair.

Straightway she screamed out against Marie, declaring her to have been in the murder. Many seemed to agree with her; De Silva for one, Darnley's father for another, and a large number of my people also. I could not bring myself to entertain such a notion, if only for the reason that such folly would be inadmissible in one who intended to rule a country. When I continued with my letter, I said so.

'For myself, I beg you to believe that I would not harbour such a thought for all the wealth of the world, nor think so badly of any Prince that breathes. I implore you to consider the matter — at once to lay your hands upon the man who had been guilty of the crime — to let no persuasion keep you from proving to everyone that you are a noble Princess and a loyal wife. I do not write thus because I doubt you, but for the love I bear towards you.'

I had it sent off at once, but it did little good, for she was set on her heedless way.

I could not credit such idiot folly. If she were indeed pregnant by Bothwell, here was her chance to smooth all over by giving Henry Darnley a kingly funeral, putting her Court into official mourning and behaving like a bereaved and sorrowing woman. By the time the child was born, folk would be quite ready to accept it as Darnley's, if she played her part correctly. Folk do forget things soon enough, being only too glad to believe comfortable explanations so that their feelings be not too upset.

But she did nothing. Darnley was not even given a state funeral, his body being left in a small house near the scene of his murder, finally being hastily buried close to Marie's father, James V, in the royal vaults. The very day after that, she went to Seton to play golf and shoot at the butts, being joined there by Bothwell himself and several of the Lords who were suspected of foul play. I learned of all this in a letter from Sir Harry Killigrew, flinging it down after I had read it, baffled at Marie's behaviour. I was relieved to hear from Matthew Lennox, imploring me to insist upon an enquiry into the death of his son, and agreed eagerly. Still naught was done in Scotland, but when the French Queen Mother, Catherine de' Medici, sent a message to tell Marie that if she did nothing to avenge her husband's death, the French royal family would not only think her dishonoured, but would be her enemies, Marie did bestir herself, fixing 12th April as a date for the enquiry.

In response to another plea from Matthew Lennox, I wrote again to Marie, requesting that she postpone the enquiry until all the evidence be thoroughly sifted, but my letter never reached her, going to Bothwell instead, who suppressed it. Yet I doubt she would have heeded it, being deaf and blind to all and any, save only Bothwell. At all events, the enquiry took place on the date given out, and to the stupefaction of all who stood by, Bothwell was exonerated from any art and part of the murder.

'God's blood, they are all in it together!' I cried, when I heard this. 'I begin to doubt her, upon my word. She acts like no innocent woman I ever knew!'

Even worse, she loaded Bothwell with gifts. She gave him jewels, money, church lands, her mother's furs, and basest of all, her murdered husband's richest garments. It was unbelievable, disgraceful; mayhap she had run mad. To think that seemed more credible than aught else, otherwise she was lost, she and her crown together.

'Mad indeed,' groaned Melville in despair.

'Blind-mad in love with Bothwell. She will neither listen to reason nor persuasion, Scotland's plight, her own standing, her son's inheritance, may all founder on the rock of Bothwell. Why, she said to me that she cared not to lose France, England and her own country for him, and would go with him to the world's end in a petticoat rather than leave him!'

'Jesu, she must be pregnant then,' I said shrewdly. 'She will have to wed him somehow, will she not? A Queen may not bear a bastard, whatever a King may do. How do they suppose to bring it about?'

'God alone knows, Madam,' answered Melville bitterly, 'and I fear He will not say.'

★ ★ ★

At last the Scottish lovers found what they considered to be a resolution of their position. Upon a journey to visit her little son, she was kidnapped at Gogar Burn, some way out of Edinburgh. There, barring her way, was the Earl of Bothwell, backed by an hundred men, all with raised pikes and swords, threatening to attack unless she came with him willingly. This of course she did, and much too willingly for her retinue to accept with equanimity. Off she galloped with Bothwell to Dunbar, where she stayed for twelve days, 'forced against her will,' as she gave out upon her return. Ravished, as she said she had been, it was necessary that she marry her seducer quickly in order to save her name in the eyes of the world. But the eyes of the world were wide open and her name already lost. No one was fooled by this shabby deception. When Bothwell made his entrance into Edinburgh leading the Queen's horse by the bridle, on 6th May, they were met by a heavy silence which should have warned them, had they ears to hear.

A few days after this farce, Marie called a meeting of her Lords, telling them that she had formally pardoned Bothwell and that she was a free agent. This caused a storm, the Lords shouting that they could never consider her free while she had aught to do with the Earl. That was her last chance to save herself. She passed it by. Even then, if she had given up Bothwell, she might have come about, that is if she could have concealed her pregnancy as others have done, and still do. It would have been difficult for a Queen, but not impossible. However, she wanted him and his child more than she cared for any other consideration, and after some judicious conniving and bribery, a divorce was obtained from Lady Jean, Bothwell's wife.

On 15th May 1567, Marie Stuart, Queen of Scots, married James Hepburn, Earl of Bothwell, in a Protestant ceremony, a bare three months after the murder of her second husband. She had married a murderer, a rapist, a bandit with no respect for women, law, property, or his country. I was appalled when Randolph told me of it, as we walked under the apple trees in the orchard at White Hall, and knew not what to say.

I had realised that this unhappy succession of events would be sure to increase the pressure upon me to wed. To forestall the inevitable, I sent my good Earl of Sussex to Austria to meet the Archduke in person. I chose Sussex because all knew of his dislike for Rob and would thus disarm suspicion, for I had no intention at all to marry. Sussex wrote me a long letter lauding the Archduke's manly perfections to the skies.

'Why, this is the Angel Gabriel himself come to earth!' I cried upon the perusal of this eulogy. 'I fear I am not good enough for such a paragon!' Reading on, I discovered that the Archduke spoke German, Spanish, Italian and Latin, and would even agree to be present at our English Protestant church services, provided that he could have a small private chapel where he alone might celebrate Mass. This was being almost too pliable. I feared I would have no reason to refuse such an accommodating prince! Then I bethought me that to have a chapel set aside for Mass might upset the more rigid of my compatriots, and seized eagerly upon this as an excuse. It was to stand me in good stead for some considerable period.

Rob, of course, was against the match, for he still wished to win me, but he put forward some cogent reasons as to why I should not wed a foreigner, one being that I would only add strength to and increase my husband's dominions, while having to subject myself to his command and lay open the secret of my Kingdom to a stranger. He also pointed out that children of foreign blood oft had an odd inter-mixture in their composition. Ha, I knew that to be true enough when I thought of my sister Mary and my cousin Marie. They both had a mighty odd inter-mixture in their compositions! So I continued to hold a watching brief in the mating game, much to the perturbation of my ministers.

In Scotland, Queen Marie's affairs were all awhirl and on a downward spiral. She commanded the return of her young son from Stirling Castle, but was told by the Lords that she could not have him while Bothwell remained by her side. Bothwell himself grew increasingly jealous of her position and their quarrels were tremendous, I heard.

I was infuriated to learn that the beautiful and expensive gold font that I had sent for Prince James's christening had been melted down, together with Marie's other plate, to use for money. She had wept bitterly over it, I was told. 'And I should think so!' I exclaimed. 'She has good reason to weep. What next will she do, by God?'

I was soon to discover. A month after their scandalous marriage, she and Bothwell left Edinburgh for Borthwick Castle, creeping out like thieves in the night. Once there, Marie commanded all her noblemen, knights, esquires, gentlemen and yeomen to meet together with enough food for six days, and all to come equipped for battle, to fight in her defence, the Lord Bothwell commanding likewise. Few answered the call, having no heart for the quarrel. Instead, the Scots Lords surrounded the castle, yelling for Bothwell to come out, calling him traitor, murderer and butcher. He slipped out of the postern gate and hid in the woods, while Marie held the Lords' attention by hurling invective upon them from the battlements. Sure, she did not lack for courage; pity it was that it were not extended in a better cause.

Du Croc did his best to achieve some sort of agreement between the Queen and her Lords, but she would have none of it and wished no agreement with any who sought to take her husband. That same evening, she dressed in men's clothes and rid out to Lord Bothwell at a meeting place arranged by them both, riding hard through the night to Dunbar, and she six months gone with child. After a week at Dunbar, she had gathered six hundred men, who were joined by over three thousand of Bothwell's men, and so it was decided to attempt to win back Edinburgh Castle. They never reached it, for the rebel Lords advanced to meet her, each side confronting the other at Carberry Hill on 15th June, a day of boiling heat causing many to swoon. Again the Lords beseeched Marie to abandon Bothwell, saying that they would call a truce if she did so. She named them traitors, while Bothwell spoke out, shouting that they were jealous of his greatness and that there was not one who would not like to be in his place! Du Croc said he showed no sign of fear, seeming bold as a lion in his peril. That was what drew her. I can understand that.

At last, while the Lords parleyed, Bothwell's men, half-dead with the heat and crazy with thirst, began to creep away into the bushes, or to drink at the edge of the nearby stream where they met friends among the rebels and joined them. The cause was hopeless and Marie realised it, sending for Kircaldy of Grange, the Lords' leader, who brought with him a flag of truce. He told her that if Bothwell would leave the field he would not be attacked, so she persuaded her husband, much against his will, to run. After catching up his unhappy wife in a desperate embrace, he called up some spearmen and rode away. They were never to meet again, those two. Each had been the downfall of the other.

Queen Marie was escorted back to Edinburgh as a captive, amid screams of hatred and foul abuse from all who came out to see her pass. She gave them oath for oath, screaming as loud as they, being lodged at last in a room of the Provost's House in the High Street. There she lay all night, with hostile throngs surging about the house, yelling for her death.

'Burn her, she is not worthy to live!' they howled. 'Kill her, drown her! Strangle the whore!'

I was aghast at this news. It seemed to me like a nightmare of the most hideous kind. I closed my eyes, almost as if to shut it out.

'She appeared at the window sundry times, your Majesty,' blurted out the messenger, kneeling in the rushes before me, the sun streaming over us both like a very mockery. 'She was in so miserable a state, her hair hanging all about her ears, and her body from the waist up all bare. She screamed and yelled at the crowd like a madwoman; I believe she knew not what she said, being hysterical with fear and shame. It was a most dreadful and piteous thing.'

'You saw this?' I breathed. 'You heard it?'

'I saw it with mine own eyes, Majesty, and with mine own ears I heard it.'

'Where lies she now?' I asked, when I could find my voice.

'At Lochleven Castle, Majesty, in the middle of a wide lake. The castle is owned by the mother of Lord James, the Earl of Moray.'

Twisting the rings on my long white fingers, I found it difficult for my mind to accept the fact that Marie Stuart, an anointed monarch, one ordained by God as Queen, should suffer such fearful degradation. Cecil, Rob, Francis Knollys, indeed all my ministers urged me to abandon her and seek the friendship of the rebel Protestant Lords. I could not do it. Whatever she had done, her Lords had sworn fealty to her in the name of God. In my eyes they were forsworn traitors, for I too was a Sovereign. I cried out that I would do all I could to assist my cousin — I promised it. I wrote to her and told her of my feelings, saying that I would be a good neighbour, a dear sister and a faithful friend. I was alone in so doing, for even the Pope had cast off my unhappy cousin. I sent Sir Nick Throckmorton off to Scotland to assure Marie of my help in restoring her to liberty in any way possible. She must pledge to renounce Lord Bothwell and punish Lord Darnley's murderers, and the little Prince James must be sent to England for me to protect him. It was the only way out that I could see.

'Tell her,' I reminded Sir Nick, 'that I engage the Prince as good safety as can be devised for any that might be even our child, born of our own body. Tell also those renegade Lords that I neither can nor will endure, for any respect, to have their Queen and Sovereign imprisoned or deprived of her estate, or put in peril of her person.'

He misliked his errand, showing a long face and moaning to all who would listen, but he followed my commands to the letter, making himself thoroughly unpopular in the process. The Scottish Lords were annoyed at my championing of their Queen and full of wonder at it. They knew not my deeper motives, nor did I wish them to know. As well as my real horror of their treatment of Marie, I would rather have seen her on her throne, Catholic though she was, managing her own problems with my help, if necessary, for these doings were naught but anarchy. What could happen in one country could happen in another, and my Northern Catholics were not famed for their cool heads. If Marie could be returned to her place through my good office, friendship with Scotland and peace among the Catholics would be assured. Besides, I had an excellent spy system all across England, ready to keep me informed if aught should run adrift in any quarter.

But no matter how I tried, her restoration was not to be. At one point her execution seemed a certainty, and I threatened bloody retribution and war if this took place. By the end of July, the attitude of the Lords appeared less fiery and death-dealing towards her, thanks to Throckmorton's unbending perseverance on my behalf. Then I heard from Melville that Marie had said that she would rather herself, as well as the Prince, be in England than anywhere else in Christendom. This was carrying things too far. To have Prince James was one thing; to have Queen Marie, dishonoured as she was, and an absolute storm-centre of troubles, was quite another, and I wrote off to Throckmorton in a fine taking, commanding him to tell her to put all such thoughts from her mind and to strive to regain her throne as peaceably as she might.

However, on 17th July, the Earl of Moray returned to Scotland and took matters in hand. He insisted upon Marie's abdication, and when she refused, confronted her with copies of certain incriminating letters that she had apparently written to Bothwell about Darnley's death. The Lords knew every word of the letters, he told her, and if she resisted abdication, he would see that the whole of Scotland knew of them also. Moreover, he said, if she refused to sign the order, civil war would result, and she and the Prince might well be assassinated. She had no chance at all to recover the Crown, he said. She wept and sobbed, being weak and ill from the birth of Bothwell's babe, and begged him not to publish those letters. She would abdicate, she said, if he would become Regent and act for Prince James while he was yet young. And so she signed three orders. One consented to the crowning of her son, the next made Scotland a Regency, the third created Lord James Regent, making him as near a King as bastard blood could be. A happy man he must have been that day.

My stars, those letters were very firebrands! I saw copies of them myself at a later date. Good God, they burned with lust, with love, with hatred, with connivance at murder. And yet they were moving, withal. She loved, never a doubt of it, no matter how wrongly. And Lord Bothwell's child was never seen. Some said twins had been born but had died, their bodies being slipped into Loch Leven's water as a grave. Some said a daughter was taken to France to be a nun there. None but Marie ever knew the truth of that sad birthing and she never spoke of it after.

So on 29th July 1567, the one-year-old Prince James was crowned King James VI of Scotland at Stirling amid scenes of great joy. I felt no such joy myself, having been out-manœuvred in such fashion by Lord James, who showed himself a low fellow when all was said and done. In later days, fearing for his precious Regency, he allowed those letters to be read aloud in Parliament for all to hear, see and examine. Copies were taken and sent abroad to all the Courts of Europe, so that everyone should understand the justification of the Scots to imprison their Queen. Even if she had not written those letters, and all believed she had, her reputation was shattered for ever by this action of her ambitious and treacherous half-brother.

★ ★ ★

It seemed to me in those days, that no sooner had I surmounted one obstacle than there was another for me to face, but I was still young enough to shrug my troubles from me with fair ease. Rising thirty-five was I in 1568, and had been a Queen for nigh on ten busy years, but I did not look my age, seeming much as I had done ten years earlier, which gave me great pleasure. My teeth were yet passable, my skin clear, white and unlined, my hair was richly red as ever, and my slimness still as a wand. Most ladies of my age looked far older, and I do not lie when I say that; it was real truth. Mayhap it was because I was ever abstemious with food and drink, eating but little and drinking of wine even less. I had it always watered for my taste. Indeed, I preferred beer or ale in moderation, rather than wine, and I was fond of water too, having it taken fresh from the many wells and springs round about London, some of which were kept especially for me. I walked a great deal also, much enjoying the exercise, for I was no Dame-Dawdler. Nay, I stepped it out as smartly as any soldier on the march, and every day too, to the dismay of my ladies.

'Tis marvellous how some things are remembered and some forgot. This middle part of my life was so full of excitement and colour and so many happenings, that they shift about and jostle in my memory, throwing up first one recollection, then another until I grow confused and fain to let all go hang and lie here like a withered old dummy with sawdust for a brain . . .

Ah, I recall that Cecil had begun his great house of Tibbals by this time and prodigious fine it promised to be, big enough for me and all my train to stay in it with comfort. He first intended it to be but a little pile for his son Robert, but it did not fall out so, being enlarged over and over again until it was an enormous palace. None of my people had to sleep under canvas by the time it was finished, and that took long enough — about twenty-five years, I believe. There are some who use the fanciful name and spelling for it, writing *Theobalds* and calling it so, but to me it was ever Tibbals and will be that same until my life's end, for I am too old now to change. There was a summer house and a great gate with a wondrous prospect to see from along the road from Waltham Cross to Cheshunt . . . Hey, but this was later, when the house was near done. Ach, how my mind swings and circles, forward and back. Old, old am I! I had not even visited the place when King Philip of Spain sent home my Ambassador in the springtime of 1568.

Ay, Dr. John Man was his name and King Philip expelled him after protesting to me about his behaviour, but without waiting for my reply, which I regarded as most high-handed. Dr. Man was accused of having abused the Pope in a loud voice for all to hear, which was scarcely diplomatic conduct, so I agreed to his recall. Unfortunately, my dear Guzman de Silva returned to Spain at about the same time. I was exceeding upset by this, seeing it as a Spanish retort for Dr. Man's churlishness, but it was not so as I discovered later. De Silva had been wishing to return to Spain for some time, because his funds had run out and he did not wish to end penniless and in debt like poor De Quadra before him. De Silva had been Ambassador to England for four years and could afford it no longer. I was heartily sorry to see him go, charming, intelligent, handsome gentleman that he was.

Before he made his final farewells, a thunderbolt burst into England in the shape of Queen Marie of Scotland. She had contrived to escape from Lochleven Castle with the aid of Lord James's young half-brother, Georgie Douglas, who had fallen deep in love with her. She managed to raise an army, but it was routed and she had to fly for her life, after witnessing the bloody slaughter of her men, fetching up at Dundrennan Abbey on the Solway exactly a year after her fateful marriage to Bothwell. From there she sent me a sorrowful letter, enclosing the heart-shaped diamond ring I had sent her in happier days as a pledge of friendship and support.

Forgetting that she had called herself the Rightful Queen of England and that there would not be room for two crowns in one realm, she crossed the Solway Firth and landed at Workington in Cumberland on 18th May, certain that I would welcome her with open arms and help her to regain her throne. Well, I wished to help and quarrelled mightily with my Councillors over the matter. I had refused to recognise Lord James as Regent, for this would acknowledge that Marie was no longer Queen, but, as De Silva pointed out to me, if I received her as Queen, then the Scottish Lords would be offended and would doubtless make trouble. If I kept her in prison, all neighbouring princes would be scandalised, he said, and if she remained free and able to communicate with her friends, great suspicions would be caused, he went on earnestly. Also, her presence would act as oil upon the banked-down fires of the Northern Catholics. What he said was truth. I realised it full well. I did not realise that he had also told my ministers that if Marie and I met, it was certain that we would not agree long together! He was probably right in that, too. But I was in a rare fix, for I had promised to stand as a sister and friend to Marie, notwithstanding. I did not dream that she would be hare-brained enough to come into England, and that was my mistake. It led me into many years of uneasiness and insecurity thereafter.

It was plain that I would have to cast personal feelings from me in this very tricky affair and view it in the light of reason and reality. Item: She had openly challenged my crown. Item: She had never ratified the Treaty of Edinburgh. Item: She had kept in touch with the Northern English Catholics, boasting of their sympathy towards her. Seen so simply, she looked to be more of an enemy than a friend, and what the very devil was I to do with her? Some of my more excitable ministers suggested a swift, secret assassination of the lady. I could not agree. Such killings were not so fashionable, nor so easily regarded as formerly, and suspicion would naturally point to me, which I did not favour. Some put forward her return to Scotland in the care of her half-brother, Lord James the Regent.

'Nay, I will not,' said I, flat. 'Nor will I send an army in her cause, so do not suggest that. Neither I nor my country will suffer it.'

'You cannot mean to let her go free, Majesty!' That was Rob. 'My God, she will be a very lodestone for disaffection up and down the country, with religion against religion!'

'Well, of course I cannot free her!' I retorted impatiently. 'But I cannot bring her to Court, neither. A pox upon the woman, she has upset all, as I am sure she does wherever she goes!'

It was resolved in a botched-up, untidy fashion in the end. Marie had been conducted to Carlisle Castle, and I sent Sir Francis Knollys, my Vice-Chamberlain, and Baron Scrope, Warden of the Western Marches, Governor of Carlisle and father-in-law to my cousin Philadelphia, to welcome her officially. Many others had welcomed her also, including hundreds of Catholics, a Scottish Bishop, various friendly noble Scottish families, and a rich merchant who had brought her thirteen yards of crimson velvet with which to make her a gown.

She had arrived with naught but what she stood up in, and had sent to ask me to supply her with gowns, jewels and ornaments. This request affected me strongly and strangely. I retired to my private cabinet, and there wept and wrung my hands for fear and anger. Everything in me revolted against parting with even one of my gowns or a single ring for her to wear. It made me feel like a child again, with none but worn and outgrown clothes, fearing each day displeasure or death as had been my lot in those far-off days. She, by her very presence, her very being in my realm, was inimical to my desperately-won security, the security which my gowns and my jewels showed like badges for all to see. It was as if she attacked the foundations of the structure I had built around myself. I could not, *could not*, send my garments, my jewels, my own property, I whimpered, beating a fist into the palm of my other hand. So I fought my battle, choking and sobbing, hunched on my bed behind the drawn tapestry curtains. Fought it and lost, I fear me, for I called Kitty Dudley to me at last, and bade her send me a tiring-wench. The wench came to my bedside and I told her to put some old, outworn garments into a box for a poor woman. That was all I had of the business, not wishing to see what she put in the box that was made ready for Sir Francis to take to Carlisle.

Well, the tiring-wench had taken me at my word and had put some old, worn things together, fit for the humble woman she thought was to receive them. Sure, they were fit rather for the dust-heap than a Queen, so I was told, and Sir Francis was most cruelly embarrassed when Marie opened the box in his presence. Lord Scrope knew not where to look, neither, for very shame, I heard, and certes it was shameful. I blamed the tiring-girl for what I called a mishap and almost believed it to be true. My other self was not so deceived, throwing me into a pet whenever Queen Marie's lack of wardrobe was mentioned. I am not proud of myself when I call that episode to mind. It showed a side of me I would fain forget. Truly the child is father of the man.

But I got the black pearls out of it, for the Earl of Moray had commandeered Marie's jewels. He knew of my love for pearls, and from the treasure he now held, had chosen six strings of beautiful pearls on knotted threads, and even more wondrous, the famous Black Pearls of France. There were over twenty-five of them, each of huge size and exactly the colour of black Muscat grapes. Catherine de' Medici wanted to buy them back, but she had no chance once I had laid eyes upon them. What was more, Lord Moray had said that I might have them at two-thirds of their value. I needed no second bidding, and in a very short time, the beautiful things were mine.

'Lord James woos us, does he not?' I laughed to Rob, admiring them hanging against my grey and silver satin gown. 'Our friendship must indeed be valuable for him to take such pains!'

★ ★ ★

Deaths there were in that year of 1568, too. Lady Catherine Grey breathed her last in January, and later in the twelve-month I lost my childhood's cherished friend and mentor, Roger Ascham, followed to Heaven but three weeks after by my beloved cousin Katey, wife to Francis Knollys. My God, she was but thirty-nine, only four years older than I. It seemed mighty young to die. I was distraught with weeping and felt I should never be comforted, unable to believe that she was truly dead and gone for ever. What I should do without her I could not tell, she had been closer than any sister I had ever known. It was dreadful, following so close upon dear Ascham's demise, for which I felt in part responsible, no matter what those who would have comforted me tried to say.

Ascham, as my Latin secretary, had been working on an ode in my honour to herald the first day of spring, sitting into the small hours to finish it in time. He caught a fearful chill in so doing, which settled in his lungs, and was gone before we fully realised he was truly ill. So loving, so conscientious, so devoted, dear, dear Roger-man. I shall not see his like again, I know it well. Many and bitter were the tears I shed as I cursed that wretched ode, wishing it had never been written. But I kept it, for all that, as a memory.

I cannot say that I shed many tears for Catherine Grey, she not having meant so much to me. She died of an affliction of the lungs also, at Cockfield Hall, Sir John Hopton's house at Yoxford. Poor soul, there were not many to mourn her. Edward Seymour did, I know, but then, he seemed to have loved her true, even though he had two wives after her. My Councillors and ministers felt it had been wise and right to constrain her, and from what I gathered from the sayings of the people, most folk felt the same. I will own that in my secret heart I did feel some unpleasant pangs of guilt, for I heard that Lady Catherine had actually wept and sorrowed herself to death. It is no easy matter to be a Queen and carry such responsibility.

For my sweet cousin Katey I paid for a magnificent funeral at Westminster Abbey, which was no less than she deserved. I felt much for Sir Francis that Katey should die while he was away in Carlisle. His was a bitter home-coming, for they were greatly devoted. Death is a fearful thing, sparing none from his icy touch, and we must all bow to his bidding in the end. But I must not go on in this wise, else I shall grow too melancholy and mayhap hasten mine own departure, God forbid! Nay, Eliza, think no more of such heavy matters, turn your mind back to the years of excitement and vitality when Lord Herries came to London from Carlisle to badger me into granting him a safe-conduct into France, to plead there for his fallen Queen.

I told him nay, nor would I give a passport to Lord Fleming neither, saying that I was not so wholly bereft of my senses as to allow the Scots Queen to introduce the French into my country. My God, that lady was a charge on me! She wrote to France, begging for an armed force that would make her Queen of

England in three months, and this while partaking of English hospitality! Well, she came to naught over that idea, despite her plots and plans. Francis Knollys had seemed much struck by her at first, to judge by his early letters, but the tone of these changed, and he deemed her a perilous nuisance, saying that all deeds were no deeds with her unless her violent appetite be satisfied, and that we should have much ado with her.

I determined that the violent appetite of my most unwelcome guest would never be satisfied, but I was as certain as Knollys that we should indeed have much ado with her. Why, it had begun already! I ordered her removal to Bolton Castle and wrote to her to be quiet and refrain from making trouble or all visits would be forbidden. I asked her to remember that she was a guest in my country and would be treated according to her station, but that she must ask no help from abroad. So she went peaceably enough to Bolton, but stirred up a veritable hornet's nest there, as we were beginning to discover was her wont.

As well as this trouble at home, I had a bothersome feeling about the Netherlands where the Duke of Alba was waging war against William of Orange. William's campaign had collapsed and I feared that

Alba might become complete master of the Netherlands, thus reaching out long, greedy fingers to England and me.

'I think it is but a matter of time,' I said to Rob as we walked arm in arm by the river at Hampton. 'I believe that one day King Philip will seek to subdue our England. He means to collect all Europe; see how he deploys his armies and works out their campaigns. He will make a bid for England at some time or other.' I broke off, seeing him fiddling with a paper. 'What have you got there that makes you to grin like a Hallow E'en turnip? Show me.'

He turned his handsome head and smiled straight into my eyes. Ah me, my Rob, so debonair, so gallant. How I loved him! That day he wore a beautiful suit of black velvet all over rubies. He had rubies in his ears and a crimson satin cap with a black feather on his dark head, and he looked past perfection itself as he smiled at me that day by the river. 'I have something for you, my lovely one,' he said, holding out the paper which was close wrapped round a small hard object. Eagerly opening the packet, I discovered a lovely jewel of a rose, all in pink enamel, on a chain for a pendant, its petals curled around a tiny mirror. The stem and the leaves were of emeralds, most delicate fair. I gasped with delight, near dropping the paper.

'Nay, do not lose the paper!' he warned me, snatching it. 'Read it; 'tis a poesie I writ for you.'

Ruefully, I began to laugh. 'Oh, Rob, I cannot do so if you hold it so far off. It is all a blur and I cannot make out the words.'

'Why not?' he asked. 'Your eyes are like any hawk, as well I know. Do not tease me, Bess. Read it.'

But I could not until I had seized the paper from his hand and approached it near to my nose. Then the words showed clear and I could read the graceful poem easily. It was the short sight that had grown upon me, forcing me to peer at my writing and my sewing, to bend over documents until my head near touched the page if the light was bad. Well, it bothered me but little, for most people of learning suffered in this wise. 'Twas all the reading by candlelight which would flicker, even though the best wax be used for the candles. Some older folk wore funnel-shaped spectacles to assist them, but I said I would be damned before I took to those. Nor I ever have to this day, and I can still make shift to see well enough.

I remember the words of that pretty rhyme

perfectly, no matter what else I have forgot in my tired old age. It was called *To My Lady Rose*. Ay, and the best of it was, I was wearing a pink satin gown with pearl trimmings and the rose pendant looked charming hanging down upon it. I did not read the rhyme aloud, but handed it back to Rob, for I wished to hear him say the words himself.

'You be my eyes, Rob,' said I persuasively. 'Read it out to me. I like it better so.'

And holding the paper, he read:

'My lady looks into a rose's heart
And there she sees, as if a part
Of that same rose, her visage fair.
A white rose she, all velvet smooth
And crown'd with fiery gold, forsooth.
She is the Rose of England, beloved in
    my sight
And in my heart, Elizabeth, my peerless
    lady bright.'

'Oh, Rob,' I sighed. 'What sweet hearing is this! Indeed, you are my Eyes, for you see me as all beautiful, which is mighty pleasant, even if it be not strictly true.'

For answer, he kissed me and I kissed him back right heartily. He thought to get his way with me that afternoon, and indeed I thought

276

he might, so forceful and passionate he grew. But we were disturbed in our arbour, for I was never alone for long.

'Word of God,' I protested, pulling down my skirts and knotting up my hair as best I could, 'you are a very Bothwell!'

At that, his sullen look changed and he roared out a-laughing so that all came running to hear the joke. They went away none the wiser, for it was between Rob and me only. And after that, I called him my Eyes — it was my little Court name for him — and oft he signed his letters and notes to me ⊙⊙, signifying eyes.

My beloved realm was growing rich; there was strong promise of power to come to my England, her dear people watched over by me who had dedicated my life to their care. All that could really disturb me was the matter of Queen Marie Stuart. I would have to swear and forswear, stifle my feelings of compassion for the unfortunate creature, harden my heart and sharpen my wits to keep her and her supporters under my thumb. It would be neither pleasant nor easy and I would be judged for it, after. But I would do it.

As to the matter of an heir, I had settled that in my own mind and there it would stay until my last moments. My people, my country, my ministers, my finances, my policies, even my pirates, all were under my careful hand and would stay under its protection as long as Elizabeth Tudor should remain on this earth.

SEVEN WEEKS MORE TO LIVE

3rd February 1603

Hey-day! I have rested snug here by the fire and I am the better for it. I feel much restored, and tomorrow will cast aside these fur wraps. I will clothe me in something lighter, brighter and more cheerful to the spirits. Mayhap I shall walk in the Long Gallery, or dance a little. It does me no manner of good to lie about. Moreover, the Venetian envoy is to visit me in a day or two, to explain why Venice has sent no Ambassador to my Court. He shall see me in my splendour and mark how state ceremonies are conducted here. I daresay it will make him open his eyes, i'faith! We shall give him something to think about, England and I.

I will continue my musings at a later date. There is much to think on and remember, much indeed. My progresses, the great Armada, my fated cousin Marie Stuart, young Essex so dear and so treacherous. Such a many memories, some beautiful, some bitter, all jostling in my old head. I will put them aside for another day, ay, another day, I do pray that there be many more left to me . . .

We do hope that you have enjoyed reading this large print book.

Did you know that all of our titles are available for purchase?

We publish a wide range of high quality large print books including:
Romances, Mysteries, Classics, General Fiction, Non Fiction and Westerns.

Special interest titles available in large print are:
The Little Oxford Dictionary Music Book Song Book Hymn Book Service Book

Also available from us courtesy of Oxford University Press:
Young Readers' Dictionary (large print edition) Young Readers' Thesaurus (large print edition)

For further information or a free brochure, please contact us at:
Ulverscroft Large Print Books Ltd., The Green, Bradgate Road, Anstey, Leicester, LE7 7FU, England. Tel: (00 44) **0116 236 4325 Fax:** (00 44) **0116 234 0205**